Kaitlin's head was spinning, and her tongue felt like sandpaper.

For the first few minutes as she began to wake up, all she could do was feel the subtle tortures within her body. And from there it only got worse.

There was a sheet covering her to her neck, but she felt funny beneath it. She was naked, and she wasn't one of those people who naturally slipped naked into bed.

A groan escaped her, and she tried to remember the evening.

It could all be explained with a single word. *Brendan*. He had arrived, and she had drained a glass of champagne in a fraction of a second. And more had followed. Then there had been dinner and cake and coffee. Irish coffee.

She hadn't been able to keep herself from telling him how good he looked. How well he had weathered time.

He'd promised not to seduce her, but he'd also warned her that he couldn't be responsible if *she* seduced him....

And, oh! The thing remember now...

Dear Reader,

I hope you've noticed our new look and that you like it as much as we do. At last, Silhouette Intimate Moments, the most mainstream line in category romance, has a look as exciting as the stories themselves. And what stories we have for you this month!

Start off with the Award of Excellence title, Linda Howard's *Duncan's Bride*. This story of a gruff rancher who advertises for a wife puts a few unexpected spins on a traditional plot. Reese Duncan wants a woman who will cook and clean and bear his children. Madelyn Patterson is willing to do all that, but she wants something in return: love. Heather Graham Pozzessere's *Wedding Bell Blues* reunites Brendan O'Herlihy with his ex-wife, Kaitlin. As best man and maid of honor for a series of weddings, they are forced to confront each other—and the feelings that have never gone away. With *Lightning Strikes*, Kathleen Korbel brings her irrepressible humor and passion to a tale of a woman who sees the future and a man who won't have a future unless he listens closely and spends it with her! Finally, Mary Anne Wilson offers *Brady's Law*. Watch as a case of mistaken identity and a tiny baby named Rocky bring together two people who never should have met but can't seem to say goodbye once they've said hello.

In months to come, watch for Emilie Richards to provide a sequel to her "sisters" stories, Lee Magner to follow *Sutter's Wife* with *The Dragon's Lair*, and favorites like Marilyn Pappano and Paula Detmer Riggs to offer new books—and all of it will be happening only in Silhouette Intimate Moments. Join us for the excitement.

Leslie J. Wainger
Senior Editor and Editorial Coordinator

HEATHER GRAHAM POZZESSERE

Wedding Bell Blues

SILHOUETTE·INTIMATE·MOMENTS®

Published by Silhouette Books New York

America's Publisher of Contemporary Romance

SILHOUETTE BOOKS
300 East 42nd St., New York, N.Y. 10017

ISBN: 0-373-07352-6

First Silhouette Books printing September 1990

HEATHER GRAHAM POZZESSERE

considers herself lucky to live in Florida, where she can indulge her love of water sports, like swimming and boating, year-round. Her background includes stints as a model, actress and a bartender. She was once actually tied to the railroad tracks to garner publicity for the dinner theater where she was acting. Now she's a full-time wife, mother of five and, of course, a writer of historical and contemporary romances.

Dedicated with love and very best wishes to all of my cousins and new cousins-in-law who were married in the past year.

Samuel DeVouno, Jr. and Janis Clems
Patrick Michael DeVouno and Andrea Hawcridde
David Kenneth Mero and Susan Mary McCarthy
Jill Marie Mero and Roman Sobocinski
Dennis Langdon Staples and Dawn Elizabeth Violette
Brent Louis Estrella and Sheryl Mallett
Howard S. Ostrout, Jr. and Lori L. Lobeda

And very especially,

Doreen Marie Law and John Tor Westermark for sharing all the laughter and the minitraumas, and for all the time we spent together, and for the sheer pleasure of seeing Derek in that tux.

And for Gail Marie Spence and James Crosbie, for having both Dennis and me (a pregnant bridesmaid) as part of it all and part of your life.

Prologue

As long as she lived, Kaitlin would never forget the day Brendan asked her to marry him. A wedding, a beautiful wedding with a white gown and all the trimmings, had been a dream of hers all her life.

And through the past three years, the dream had always included Brendan.

He proposed with style. With the same style that had attracted her from the beginning, with the handsome appeal and charisma that had swiftly and surely convinced her that it was not puppy love, with the tenderness that had proved to her that there was much, much more between them than young passion and, as her mother warned, growing hormones.

No, she was in love with him.

And he was in love with her. The forever kind of love, the "'til death do us part" kind of love. A lifetime of commitment, of vows, of promises, pure and bright and shining forever.

In years to come she would remember the night and the picture they made together. He had reached his full height of a solid six foot two, and his shoulders were powerful and squared, and still he seemed lean, both mature and youthful. And with the straying lock of ebony hair that fell over his eyes, he was handsome enough to attract the attention of women of all ages. She had known that she was shining that night, too. Shining with excitement.

She had always been delighted that he was hers. The quarterback of the high school football team, the captain of the debating team, somehow managing to convey a certain sexy wildness while maintaining an average very close to a perfect 4.0. And from the moment they had met, their eyes locking despite the length of the hallway between them, their relationship had seemed fated.

She'd known who he was, of course. Everyone at school did. And he had smiled. Slowly. With cocky assurance. And his gold-flecked emerald gaze had swept the length of her. That had been slowly, too.

And then he had turned away, with utter confidence. She would be there when he was ready for her, the gesture seemed to say.

Kaitlin had never had any intention of being anyone's easy conquest. And neither did she need to be.

From her grandmother she had inherited her rich, beautiful strawberry blond hair. Hair that rippled and waved down the length of her back, soft and abundant. She had her grandmother's startling blue eyes, too, light, crystalline and clear. And her Irish complexion, soft and creamy, with rose-tinted cheeks. She was her mother's daughter, too, determined, bright, savvy... and nicely built.

So at the first dance of the year, she was a flirt. A terrible flirt. She laughed outrageously. She moved as if she was dancing on air. She teased the boys mercilessly but grandly, and...

And she kept her eyes on Brendan. But he didn't come near her. Not until the last dance was announced, and then she was suddenly in his arms, and he was staring at her.

"Are you happy, Kaitlin? That whole pack of lost puppies is over there tripping over their hanging tongues. You've set their self-confidence back a decade."

"Oh, have I?" she challenged him. But something in his eyes was very serious, even though he was still offering her his slightly mocking smile. "I was dancing, that's all. Enjoying the night."

"Teasing every guy here to distraction."

"Really? Well, if you don't mind, then, Brendan, let me go, and I won't be teasing anyone any longer."

He shook his head. "No more, Kaitlin. You're with me now because you want to be. Because you want me."

She had smiled disdainfully at his sheer effrontery. "I want you? Don't be so certain."

"But I am. You'll always go after what you want, Kaitlin. And right now, you want me."

"You're awfully egotistical, Brendan O'Herlihy—" she began. Then his lips were suddenly on hers, and he kissed her. The kind of kiss she'd never dared imagine. Open-mouthed, hot, demanding, coercive, a kiss that stole her breath away. She could barely hear the music; she could barely stand. She forgot what she had been saying.

Then the kiss ended, and when she looked into his eyes, she knew that her world had changed. He smiled again, gently. Assured, mature, certain.

"You're where you belong right now," he told her softly. "And it's where you're staying."

"But I—I might be teasing you," she stammered.

He shook his head. "No. Because whatever you promise me, Kaitlin, you will give."

She had meant to jerk away from his arms, but she never did. She met his eyes, saw the challenge there, and they danced until long after the music had stopped.

From that moment on, they were one.

Oh, they fought. She *was* something of a flirt, and he was possessive and had a rather infamous temper. And she was jealous. Jealous as she had never thought she could be in her life. But there was no one quite so fascinating. No one quite so startlingly handsome. No one with enough casual, masculine charm to sweep away an entire class. Girls liked Brendan. She knew that half her classmates—half of her good "friends"—were just waiting for them to break up so they could have a chance at him.

But despite the wild fights and her continual determination to prove that she was her own woman, they never did split up. Not for a weekend. Not even for a day.

By her eighteenth birthday they had been together for three years. For the occasion, Brendan had rented a small suite at an old hotel in the country. He had ordered up dinner and even thought to see that there were flowers and candles on the table, and that everything was as elegant as possible.

She had worn a strapless sea-green satin dress, and they had shared a bottle of white wine across the candlelit table.

And then he had stood up and taken her into his arms. She had known, on that night, that they were going to make love.

Everyone who had dated as long and as steadily as they had had already done so. Her interest had certainly been piqued; she was both eager and scared. She'd heard stories from her friends about awkwardness and pain and frenzied groping—and the back seats of old cars.

But she should have known that it would be nothing like that with Brendan.

His kiss was something she already knew well. Deep and searing, hot and passionate, soul-stealing. And the exquisite, shivery feeling as his lips moved down the length of her throat was also something she knew.

But always before, there had been a certain restraint.

Not this night.

She was swept into his arms and carried through the living area of the suite to the bedroom, where he placed her on the queen-size bed. He lay down beside her and kissed her again, then showered her shoulders with searing tongue strokes that left her quivering in their wake.

At last he found the zipper of the sea-green dress and slid it down. And where the material of the dress parted, the lightest caress of his lips followed. She never quite realized how, but suddenly the dress was gone, and then he just stopped and stared at her, drawing his breath in very sharply before he touched her. Her lacy strapless bra was shell pink, as were her panties and her elegant little garter belt. He had seen her in less, actually, since he had seen her in the half dozen bikinis she had owned over the past few years. But it didn't seem to matter when he moved again and whispered that the garter belt was the sexiest thing he had seen in his entire life. Then he tossed aside her shoes, and she was amazed when he clutched her foot and teased her flesh through her sheer stocking, massaging, kissing her arch and then her ankle, the length of her calf, the back of her knee and along her thigh, before stripping the stocking away. And when he repeated the process with her other leg, she found herself shivering as if she was frozen, even while her skin was flaming from his touch.

She was hot. Hot as she had never been in all her life, barely able to keep still, to think, to comprehend. There would be nothing for her tonight except sensation...touch...the feel of his lips against her naked flesh.

Once her stockings were gone, her bra was next. He nuzzled her breasts tenderly and gently, and then he told her that he had been wrong before. The garter belt was something, but nothing in the world was as erotic as her breasts. He kissed each one in turn, starting slowly, then moving inward with erotic, soft flicks of his tongue until he surrounded the hardening rosy center and swept it into his mouth, creating a startling fire that left her moaning and thrashing restlessly beside him.

It burned deep in the center of her, hot and aching, there, at the juncture of her thighs.

Always he touched her, always he seared her. Kissed and whispered. The garter belt came next, and then the shell-colored lace panties. And his touch moved closer and closer to the fire, until he stroked the flame itself, igniting her, causing her to cry out in soft, incomprehensible whispers. He rose to remove his own clothing, and in the shadows he was magnificent, tall and broad-shouldered, lean and hard, and when he lay beside her, he was all hot, rippling muscle, smooth and sleek and beautiful. And he was more. He was the man she loved. Had loved for all these years. And she knew that she would love him forever.

His body moved over hers, and she gasped, startled at the feel of him.

She had thought she knew him so well....

But she hadn't quite known this part of him. Huge, throbbing, arrogant against the bare flesh of her thigh, threatening, promising, warm against the gates of her femininity.

But she did know his voice. Heated, intense, passionate. Encouraging...telling her that she should touch him, too.

She did so, nearly crying aloud at the vital heat of him. And then she was burying her face against his shoulder, amazed that when she had touched him, the fire within her had grown. She ached. She wanted him. She needed him.

But he waited. Waited for the words of need to come tearing from her throat. And when they did, he entered at last. Slowly, carefully, tenderly. When the first startled cry of pain came to her lips, he whispered and held still, then slowly moved again. Kissing her. Touching her. Until the delicious feelings returned again. Until the ache became a drumbeat, a pounding, a pulse. Something nearly desperate. So sweet and searing that it was agony, and so exquisite that it was ecstasy. She felt herself climbing, flying, reaching the clouds, where at last the sweetness exploded within her like the bursting of the sun in the sky. Hot, melting rays swept through her body, filling her with molten honey and sensations of love and warmth beyond anything she had ever imagined.

The heat, she thought, was him. Filling her. And it was wonderful, because she knew that she had not reached that searing splendor alone, that she had been everything he had wanted, that he had filled her, been a part of her, and would be, from now until forever.

Even afterward, it was beautiful. He pulled her close into his arms and held her tenderly, smoothing back her damp hair and whispering softly that he loved her.

The night was still young, and it became a time for explorations. They bathed together, and made love in the shower. She began by pressing sensual kisses against his chest, nipping at his shoulders and back, and stroking his hard, muscled buttocks as the shower cascaded over them. Even when they were ready to leave, they couldn't quite bear it. She wrapped her arms fiercely around his neck, and he backed her against the wall, lifting her until she locked her legs around him, and they made love right there, standing up. And it was as passionately fulfilling as before.

She would never be the same, she knew. Never.

He had told her many times through the years that he loved her. But now, somehow, that love seemed so complete. They had shared the secret of their intimacy. No one could know the depths of their love.

It was two weeks later that he asked her to marry him. And he did it with the same careful thought and love and tenderness.

They were out with her family, at the annual spring dinner in Petersham, and he had led her out to the porch, where they could be alone. He'd seated her on the wicker swing, and the rich beauty of the new season surrounded them. There were birds above them in the trees, and flowers everywhere. The breeze was soft and caressing, and sunlight poured down upon them.

To her amazement, he was suddenly on his knees. Brendan, so handsome in his suit, so masculine, and grinning just a little, was kneeling as he took her hands in his. She trembled, remembering what it was like to make love with him, and he spoke the words that were so simple, so traditional.

"Kaitlin, I love you. And I want you to be my wife. I want us to spend our lives together. Will you marry me?"

She stared at him, her eyes growing wider and wider, and then she screamed and threw her arms around him. She didn't care whether anyone came on them while they were kissing so passionately, out there on the porch. Not her little cousins, not her mother, not even her father.

But no one came out. And eventually they were sitting together on the swing, and he flicked open a jewel case.

It held a diamond ring.

It wasn't huge, but it was the most beautiful ring Kaitlin had ever seen. The stone was set in a simple gold scroll, and Brendan explained that the wedding ring would surround it, completing the design, two entwined roses.

He slipped the ring on her finger, and she leaned back, unable to stop admiring it, and rested her head on his shoulder.

Then they started to dream.

College was ahead of them, but Brendan wasn't worried about that. He had earned a scholarship to the school of marine biology in Miami, and, beyond that, he had a trust fund that his bootlegging grandfather had left him. And her parents would be willing to help, too; college had always been important to them. Of course, they would both work, too, preferably on campus. They would manage. They would manage very well.

She wasn't concerned about the future, although she knew her father would be. But her father liked Brendan, had always liked him. He liked the fact that Brendan had only touched liquor sparingly, and he liked the fact that Brendan had always seemed to listen and weigh and watch before coming to a decision. Her parents wouldn't mind. They would understand.

It was the immediate future that fascinated Kaitlin.

"Oh, Brendan! Can we have a big wedding? Everyone in both our families? Everything?"

He laughed. "I think you're more excited about the prospect of the wedding than you are about being married. But we'll have whatever you want. You've always known how to smile and tease and come after whatever you want, Kaitlin."

"All I want is you."

"And the biggest wedding in the world."

She shook her head and touched his cheek; her eyelashes were damp. "No! I can't think of anything that I'd rather do than wake up beside you every day of my life. But I'll never forget my Aunt Gwen's wedding. It was the most beautiful thing I'd ever seen. She had three flower girls and five bridesmaids, and there were flowers and candles everywhere, and they wrote their own vows, and she was so beautiful in that white wedding gown. Oh, Brendan, I want it all, the train halfway down the church, the music and the flowers—especially the flowers!"

He hugged her tight. "It's fine with me. Except that I think I'd better work this summer, then. I'm not sure your parents can pay for all that, even if you are an only daughter." He smiled, and she laughed and promised that she intended to work hard, too. After all, it was her dream.

But he was still Brendan. The Brendan she had fallen in love with, the one she had battled and adored for what already seemed like her entire life. He was her secret lover, her pride, her delight. And she knew the depth of his love for her.

"We'll have everything," he promised her. "Everything you want. The long white gown with a train so long the guests will have to be careful not to trip on it. And we'll have champagne, and candles, and most of all, we'll have flowers. So many flowers that we'll be smelling them for the first ten years of our marriage.''

''And I'll be your wife, and I'll take your name, and we'll live happily ever after,'' she vowed in return.

Brendan spoke to her father, and they announced their engagement that very night.

They even managed to slip away alone together, for at least an hour, to a beautiful old inn on the Vermont side of the border. As they made love, they spoke of their love again. He promised to love her forever, and she vowed that she would always be there for him.

And he meant the promise that he made to her. He meant to give her everything. Just as she meant to keep her vow.

But fate did not intend for it to be.

In time, she would take his name.

But she was not going to walk down the aisle in a long white gown.

Nor were they going to live happily ever after.

Often, in the years ahead, Kaitlin would be glad of that time. She would look back on the girl she had been, on the broken promises and shattered dreams. And she would think, *At least I had that day.*

And the really funny, yet horribly painful, thing was that she still loved him.

The shining glimmer of love, of that dream, would never quite go out.

Chapter 1

Twelve years later...

The fact that Kaitlin first misunderstood her grand-mother was entirely her own fault.

They had gone out to breakfast together, just as they did every Wednesday morning. But the Seashell Sunblock commercial presentation had to be given to the company VIPs that afternoon, and even though Kaitlin was prepared, she was restless. This was her own ad agency, and the account was a very important one. And the verdict had just come in on a particularly scandalous assault trial and she couldn't help but notice the headlines on the *Miami Herald*, so she was reading the story out of the corner of her eye when Gram first spoke.

"Kaitlin, I'm going to be mur—"

Mur—and something garbled. It didn't help any that after fifty years in this country Gram still spoke with a brogue so strong it could be sliced clean through with a knife.

Mur-something. Gram was going to be mur-somethinged. That was all Kaitlin heard. She looked up, but Gram was looking down. It had sounded very much as if she had said, "Kaitlin, I'm going to be murdered."

Murdered. Well, it was natural that Gram would be nervous. She was nearly seventy, and alone. She had refused to live with Kaitlin, who had offered her separate living quarters on her own property. Gram liked the condominium where she lived; the building was filled with other active retirees. She missed children, of course. Gram loved children, and she missed them when she was in Florida. But she went north every winter to spend the holidays with the family. She had ten great grandchildren, aged eight months to eighteen years, to greet her lovingly on each visit. Gram was precious to all of them. She was their link; she was, in essence, the Ireland of their ancestry. She told wonderful stories, and when Kaitlin had been a little girl, Gram had her really believing in leprechauns and convinced that if men practiced evil deeds, the banshees, the wailing death ghosts of Eire, might really come for them.

So, with her brogue, she was difficult to understand at best. But then, that big hairy German shep-

herd of hers had eaten her best set of teeth, and Gram
hated the new ones, said they didn't fit right.

So she was afraid of being killed. There had been a
rash of robberies—home invasions, they called them
now—and it was natural that she should be fright-
ened.

"Oh, Gram!" Kaitlin said. She took Gram's hands
in her own. "Now, listen to me. You are not going to
be murdered. This is a very scary world that we live in,
but you're really not going to be murdered. Gram, if
you want, you can come and stay with me, just for a
while—"

"And I'll be damned if I do, that I will!" Gram
said, her tone surprised—and her words startlingly
clear. She was still such a beautiful woman, small,
with brilliant blue eyes. And she kept her hair a very
attractive silver-blue color. She still looked as sweet as
a saint, and to hear such a statement come so explo-
sively from her seemed quite an irony.

"But if you're afraid of being murdered—"

"I didna say 'murdered,' Kaitlin O'Herlihy. I didna.
You didna listen to me."

Kaitlin folded her hands on the table. She tried not
to glance at her watch; she would be at work in plenty
of time, and this—whatever it was—seemed important to her grandmother. She lowered her head, smiling with a certain relief. "I'm sorry, Gram. What *were*
you saying?"

"Kaitlin, I'm going to be married. Not murdered—what did you think, that I'd become a hysterical old recluse? Married, Kaitlin. Married."

"Married!"

Kaitlin couldn't have been more stunned if her grandmother had been absolutely certain that she was going to be murdered in the next five minutes.

Married . . .

Gram, married?

She'd been a widow for nearly forty years. She'd raised five children on her own in a new country, and she'd gone these many, many years without even dating.

And now she was going to be married.

Kaitlin's jaw wouldn't quite work. Then she managed to repeat the word. "Married?"

"Married, young lady. Aye, now you've heard me right," Gram said with a sigh. "And shut your mouth, love. People will start staring at us."

Kaitlin didn't know whether to smile or laugh or worry. Then she managed to say, "But, Gram, you haven't even been dating—"

"Oh, but I have. And I didna say a word to you or your mother or any of your cousins, because I didna intend to take the likes of the teasin' you'd all be givin' me. But I've been seeing Mr. Rosen every week at bingo for over a year now. And we've been meeting Sunday night for dinner, and going to the theatre and movies and—"

"Rosen? Gram, is he a Jewish gentleman?"

"Aye, that he is. And don't you be sayin' a word about it to me, Kaitlin O'Herlihy. At me age, it just don't seem to matter anymore. He's got a beautiful house by the water, and we're going to move into it. And we'll have Hanukkah candles and a Christmas tree, and don't ye dare be sayin' a word to me about it, eh, Kaitlin?"

She was going to laugh. She was going to burst into laughter. She could remember how terrified they had all been to go to Gram and tell her that Kaitlin's cousin Mary Elena was going to marry outside the church— and Lance Hendricks was merely a Lutheran.

"Kaitlin—" Gram warned.

She caught her grandmother's hands again. "Gram, I'm delighted."

And then the tough determination that had brought her through many years of hardship left Gram's eyes, and a charming, girlish uncertainty filled them. "Are you certain, Kaitlin? Will the family mind? I've not even told me sons and daughters yet."

"They'll be thrilled," Kaitlin promised her. And then she laughed again. "Gram, you little devil, you. All this activity, and we didn't know a thing. It's wonderful. Absolutely wonderful. When is the big occasion? And when do I get to meet Mr. Rosen?"

"This weekend, for dinner, Kaitlin. I thought that maybe you wouldn't mind having something small at your house."

Kaitlin grinned. "Not a bit. I'll be delighted. When is the wedding?"

"Two weeks from now. At the Lotus Gardens. Justice of the Peace Merkin has promised to wed us, and both Rabbi Nathan and Father Tangini have promised to bless the ceremony."

"How wonderful!"

"Aye, Kaitlin. And I'm countin' on you, girl, that I am. Will you stand by me?"

"Be your witness?"

"My maid of honor."

"Oh, Gram, of course! But what about your daughters, or your friends—"

"You're family, Kaitlin. Me daughters will understand. You're the one who's looked after me down here all these years, don't ye be denyin' it. I want you with me when I wed Mr. Rosen. Will you stand for me?"

"Of course! I'd be honored, Gram! I'll charge right into it. The Lotus Gardens! It will be beautiful. Have you chosen a dress yet?"

For the remainder of the meal they planned a night to shop for dresses, then a night to go by the florists, then a day to find the proper cake.

Kaitlin was thrilled, although for a moment it was there—a tiny little jab of pain in the center of her heart. It always came, despite the pleasure she often felt for others. She loved weddings, but things just . . . Sometimes they just still hurt.

Then the pain ebbed away. She'd never been bitter and she'd never been jealous. And she loved Gram almost as deeply as she loved her own mother. This was funny, sweet, charming—and wonderful. Nothing in the world seemed quite as wonderful as getting to help plan her grandmother's wedding.

Kaitlin forgot her commercial until she happened to glance at her watch. Then she was truly sorry that she was going to have to leave. "Gram, where can I drop you? I've got to get to work."

Gram didn't want to go anywhere; she wanted to stay in the mall and maybe buy "a wee bit of new under-type things." Kaitlin smiled, kissing her good-bye and watching her disappear into a throng of shoppers. She looked great, Kaitlin decided. Truly radiant. Just like a bride. A beautiful woman with those ageless eyes and her wonderful peaches-and-cream complexion. And after all these years . . .

Kaitlin seemed to float in to work on her grandmother's euphoria. Janis Epstein, her assistant, was waiting in her office, gathering together the storyboards for the presentation. "Hey, boss." Janis grinned. "I thought you'd be early today. Worried, chomping away at those nails of yours."

Kaitlin made a face and set her handbag beneath her desk. "Janis, guess what?"

"What?"

"My grandmother is getting married."

Janis's brows shot up with surprise, then she laughed. "Married! I didn't even know she'd been out on a date!"

"Neither did I," admitted Kaitlin. Janis handed her a cup of coffee, and she sat in her chair for a moment, telling Janis all about her grandmother's plans.

Janis clicked her tongue. "Can you imagine? All of us, supposedly in our primes—or semi-primes, at least!—out there looking for Mr. Right, and Lizzie Boyle sweeps him right out of a bingo game. Can you imagine?"

Kaitlin grinned and admitted that it was tough to picture.

Then Janis jumped up. "Hey, we've got about ten minutes before we need to show up in the boardroom."

"Um. And face Mr. Harley," Kaitlin admitted. "I'm rushing into the ladies. I just need two seconds."

The "ladies" was actually her private bath in the corner of her office. She went in quickly, drawing her brush from her handbag even as she did so. In the mirror above the handsome marble sink, she surveyed her reflection. Not bad, she reflected. Not when she had turned the corner this year and celebrated her thirtieth birthday just a month ago.

She smiled suddenly, wondering if she would grow old like Gram. Maybe she would, with luck. She still possessed a headful of wild strawberry blond hair, thick, wavy hair that curled around her shoulders and halfway down her back. Today it was all neatly tied into a French braid, to complement her deep maroon paisley skirt and loose blouse. It was an outfit that was all business but still very feminine. Her eyes, she thought, were her best feature, wide and light blue. She had Gram's skin, too. Maybe she *would* age well. So far, she assured herself, she hadn't done too badly for thirty. The company was hers. Eventually she wanted to make Janis a partner, just so that she could have more spare time. She had a good reputation in the business, and she worked very hard and loved it.

The only thing that she didn't have at thirty, the only thing...

Was anything that resembled a personal life, she told herself dryly.

Well, she reminded herself, she hadn't wanted a personal life, had she?

She smoothed back the loose strands of hair over her forehead and applied a little lipstick, then decided that she was as presentable as she was going to be.

She turned out the light and headed back through her office. She was just about to leave the room when she heard her personal line buzz. She picked up the receiver to tell Samantha that she'd have to call whoever it was back, but before she could say anything, Samantha spoke quickly.

"It's your cousin Donna from Massachusetts. She says she just needs two seconds. Is that all right?"

"Yeah, fine, thanks, Sam." She pushed the extension button on the phone. Donna would understand her need for haste, and if she wanted to say something, it must be important.

"Donna, hi, me. I am in a hurry, but—"

"I know, I know. Seashell Sunblock, right?" Donna didn't wait for an answer; she plunged on. "Kaitlin, I'm getting married."

"Married?" Kaitlin gasped. Married, the same as Gram had told her. Donna had all her teeth—there was no mistaking the word for "murdered" this time.

Kaitlin shut her mouth. How many times had she already said that word—and as stupidly—today? She recovered much more quickly this time. "Oh, Donna, that's wonderful. Congratulations."

"Thanks."

"Bill?" Kaitlin asked hesitantly. The last time she had spoken with Donna, they had been going through a rocky patch, even though they were both great people. Kaitlin had known Bill Piccolo all her life and liked him very much.

Bill would have been in her own wedding. If there had been a real wedding.

The little jab of pain was sharper this time. She exhaled and willed it away.

"Yes, Bill, who else?" Donna said. Then she rushed on. "I just wanted to tell you now because I couldn't stand waiting. I'll let you go, and I'll talk to you tonight. Kaitlin, I want you to be my maid of honor. Will you think about it, please?"

"It's an honor. I don't need to think about it," Kaitlin assured her. "But when is it? We've got time, don't we? You're never going to believe this, but I'm standing up for someone else."

"Who?" Donna asked.

"Gram."

"Gram!" Donna shouted over the wires. "Gram?"

"Yes, Gram. Don't say anything, though. She just told me this morning, and I'm sure she wants to tell the aunts and uncles herself."

"Why, that little devil!"

"That's exactly what I said, and straight to her face!" Kaitlin agreed. "She's being married very quickly, though—she says she doesn't want to waste time at her age, or something like that. Anyway, she can tell you, which I'm sure she'll do."

"She'll get to her grandchildren after she makes it through all her children!" Donna laughed. "But no, we won't be married right away. We've got an awful lot of planning to do. Thanks for saying you'll be my maid of honor. Now hurry up, knock 'em dead, and I'll talk to you later. Oh, Kaitlin, I'm so excited!"

"Right, talk to you soon," Kaitlin promised, and hung up the phone.

But she didn't rush out of the room. Instead she stared at the receiver. First Gram and now Donna. It was wonderful. She loved both of them dearly. And they were both asking her to be a part of their joy.

She couldn't even blame it on the water. They didn't live in the same cities.

Seashell Sunblock, she reminded herself sternly. She marched out of her office and down the hall.

In the conference room, Mr. Garrett Harley, president and chairman of the board of Seashell Products, was already seated at the long mahogany table, with Tom Pinchon, his promotions man, and his sister, Netty Green, the VP.

"Good morning." Kaitlin greeted them all, sweeping into the room with a broad smile. The storyboards were already set up in the front of the room, and Janis had seen to coffee and ashtrays. Garrett Harley, forty-five and broad as a barn, but smart as a whip to have put Seashell Products where it was, grunted. Netty, older and much, much thinner, murmured a thin-lipped reply, and Tom nodded.

This was not a cheerful group, Kaitlin reminded herself. It never had been. There wasn't going to be any light, comfortable repartee in the room today, so she might as well plunge in. Janis was standing in the back of the room, ready to give her silent support. Kaitlin walked straight to the storyboard to make her pitch.

"Mr. Harley, you told me that you want your new sunblock to appeal to the young men and women flocking the beaches. Since there's been so much publicity about the dangers of the sun, we didn't want to concentrate on the product's tanning qualities, but rather on its protective virtues."

"I told you to sell sex," Harley said. He looked at his sister and said flatly, "Sex sells."

"Harley, I won't have anything lewd," Netty began irritably.

Kaitlin quickly interrupted her. "I think we have a commercial that you'll both like very much. It's sexy, but not lewd, I promise.'' She flashed a smile to Netty, whose face didn't seem to crack.

Harley, however, grinned broadly. "Let's see it."

Kaitlin showed them her first picture. "We've got a nice couple on a beach. A really good-looking couple."

"Not kids," Netty protested.

"No, not kids," Kaitlin said. Then she grimaced inwardly at the term she was about to use. "Yuppies. Late twenties, early thirties. She's in a two-piece suit, as you see here—"

"Not one of those string things," Netty said.

"No, just a nice two-piece, a very decent bikini, I promise you. I know just the suit I want—my artist has sketched it here, as you can see." She pointed to the picture. "Now, Mr. Harley, this couple may be a little bit older than what you first had in mind, but they're very good-looking, and sexy. And old enough and mature enough to be affluent, to vacation in the Caribbean and Bermuda and Cozumel. So here they are, together on the beach. And the narrator is saying, 'When you touch her this afternoon...'" Kaitlin quickly moved on to the next picture, where the man was smoothing lotion over the woman's back. "'Touch her with Seashell Sunblock...'" Then she flipped another page, and the same couple was shown dancing beneath the moon, "'to be sure you can touch her tonight.'"

There was one last picture. Kaitlin flipped the page. The man was sweeping the woman into his arms and carrying her into an attractive hotel room. Sexy, but absolutely not explicit. Kaitlin had discarded idea after idea until she and Janis had come up with this one. And she was sure they had it just right.

But Harley was quiet for several long, long moments. Netty merely sat with her lips pursed, and it seemed that Tom didn't dare say a word until one of them spoke.

Then Harley slammed his hand against the table and pulled a plump cigar from his coat pocket. "I like it! By golly, I like it." He swung around to Netty. "Well, Netty?"

Kaitlin held her breath. Then Netty nodded slowly. "Except, of course, that I want to see these people when you've chosen the actor and actress. I don't want youngsters out there, truly, I don't."

"Netty, I promise, I'll make them both thirty," Kaitlin swore solemnly.

"And I want to see the bathing suit."

"I've got a picture in my office." She glanced at Janis, who didn't need to hear a word. She quickly left the conference room, and returned with the picture while they discussed media other than television and the way the campaign might be modified.

Netty seemed pleased, and Garrett Harley seemed pleased, so Tom seemed pleased, too. They shook hands all around.

Samantha brought in the contracts, which were promptly signed, and everyone shook hands again.

And then finally—finally!—Harley and crew were gone.

"Blessed Mary!" Kaitlin exclaimed, falling back into the swivel chair at the head of the table, then hopping up to hug both Samantha and Janis. "We did it! No muss, no fuss. We've got it! The Seashell commercial! Sam, call Danny in here. We've got to celebrate. There's a bottle of champagne in my fridge—I bought it just in case. Get Danny, and we'll have a toast."

Sam, grinning, ran out. Danny was Kaitlin's artist, an amazing young man who could create beautiful illusions and more—he could understand everything going on in Kaitlin's mind and get it on paper.

Janis shook her head. "I don't believe we did it!" Then she wagged a finger at Kaitlin. "And you almost blew it. Boy, was Harley getting edgy when you didn't walk in here precisely on the hour. What happened? Nothing bad, I hope?"

"No. My cousin is getting married, too. Donna. In Massachusetts. And I'm going to be her maid of honor."

Janis arched a brow. "Your grandmother and your cousin, all in one day? Maybe it's in the water," she said, echoing Kaitlin's original thought. Then she sighed wistfully. "Wish *I* could drink some of that stuff."

"Don't you dare. I'm going to need you here. I'm going to have to go back and forth to Massachusetts a few times, I'm sure."

"Never fear, Janis is here," she teased. Then her eyes widened. "No, wait, go right ahead, fear away. Panic, in fact! You *are* going to see to this commercial shoot before you leave, right? Oh, please, say right!"

"We've got Harley in the bag, and I plan to shoot by the end of the week. I want to shoot right on the beach, and we'll use Addison's Resort. I've already made a few tentative arrangements. It's elegant and has beautiful rooms. I'll guarantee everything this afternoon. And I'll call the talent agency and reserve the models I want. I already asked for Mark Ford and Cissy Grissom. They should be perfect. This is going to be perfect. Perfect! I don't see a problem in the world."

And she believed it. When Danny came in, she hugged him fiercely, then managed a bit of a speech telling them all that they'd accomplished a tremendous coup, sweeping Seashell Products away from some really hefty competition.

That afternoon she was able to make all the arrangements, and that night, she took the whole crew to dinner, where she drank more champagne, forgetting until she got home that champagne gave her an awful headache.

In the morning, she awoke with too many memories.

So, Gram was getting married.

She, at least, was having the decency to go through a small and simple ceremony.

But Donna's wedding . . .

Donna's would be sumptuous. Kaitlin's beautiful, dark-haired cousin would make a stunning bride. She'd wear a long white gown, just as Kaitlin had always dreamed of doing.

Well, Kaitlin told herself, that dream was over now. She could never dress in white, that was certain. And she had no right to envy Donna; she had already been a bride. She'd never had the wedding of her dreams, but she *had* been a bride.

What were dreams, anyway?

Nothing but crystal illusions to be shattered. The wedding she and Brendan had promised one another had never come about. Brendan's cousin had been killed in an automobile accident, and the wedding had been called off.

That hadn't mattered then. To all of them, Sean had been all that mattered.

She would never forget going to see Brendan the day after Sean had died, and she would never forget the funeral. Brendan's cousin Sean would have been his best man; the two had been best friends forever. Brendan hadn't cried. He had just stood there in the pouring rain, in the gray of the day, staring at the coffin where Sean lay. She'd been there. At his side. She'd cried for Sean, and she'd cried again that night. Her father had held her and told her that that was the worst part of growing up, the death of love and friendship and innocence. The death of dreams. Meeting the reality of life.

For Brendan, it had been a death of innocence indeed. After that he hadn't wanted to see Kaitlin. He should have been clinging to her; she should have been comforting him. But no one could reach him.

And then she'd gone away to school, while Brendan had stayed at home. She'd never stopped loving him, but she hadn't been able to reach him. And when he had enrolled in January, he had been different. Brooding, quiet, angry. Always angry. But she hadn't stopped loving him. . . .

He had hurt her, though, and she had wanted to hurt him in return. He'd said that he was ready to plan the wedding again, but even as she called the caterers and tried to make arrangements long distance, something was unraveling on her. They nearly lived together. They continued to make love, wildly, passionately. But she didn't seem able to touch him anymore.

And then one night he didn't show up when he was supposed to. James Brager did, though. James was one of Brendan's best friends, and that night he was so sweet and so good to her that she found herself pouring out her heart to him. And then James kissed her. There was no passion in it, just friendship.

But Brendan, who had shown up at last, didn't see it that way.

She would never forget how his eyes had looked that night. Fierce. Burning. There had been something about his face that had reminded her of the day he had stood by the grave, at Sean's funeral. Another death of innocence, Kaitlin's father might have said. She could have given him an explanation, but Brendan didn't want it. Not after he'd walked in and found them together. His rage had been terrible, and the fight that followed even worse. The shouting, the things they said. Until he had tossed her on the bed and made love to her in a frenzy. She had fought at first, but then she had clung to him, praying that they could get back something of the love they'd known....

But they hadn't. He had left. And the next thing she knew, he had volunteered for the Navy.

And then she found out about the baby.

Kaitlin rose, ignoring her headache, suddenly more aware of the agony of memory than of any present pain. She staggered into the bathroom, took two aspirin and decided that she looked every bit of her thirty years. No, she looked more. Much, much more.

She called the office and said she would be late. Sam sounded unhappy—as if she wished she could have called in late, too.

Oh, well, there were some advantages to being the boss, Kaitlin thought.

She started perking coffee, planning the shoot in her head. Then the phone rang, and she answered it. It was another one of her cousins, this one local. Soon after Kaitlin had graduated, Barbara had come south and lived with her for several years before falling in love and eventually moving in with her beloved down the street. Joe was another transplant from Massachusetts, and he had gone to the university, then fallen in love with the sunlight and the South and stayed on. He was a musician with one bad marriage behind him, but Barbara stayed with him, believing in her heart that one day Joe would realize that she was a very different woman from his ex-wife, and marry her and raise a family with her.

They had been living together for six years. Kaitlin had to give Barbara credit for tenacity. It had taken Joe two years to let her move in, another two for him to allow her to bring in any furniture. Now it seemed they were married, they were such a normal couple. They were happy, and Kaitlin knew that Joe really loved her cousin. He just had difficulty with the marriage idea.

"Hey, Barbara, how'd you know I'd be home?" Kaitlin asked.

"'Cause I called the office," Barbara said. There was an edge of excitement in her voice, but Kaitlin's head was pounding and she was busy plugging in the coffeepot, and she didn't hear it. "You delinquent," Barbara accused. "What did you do? Go out drinking champagne?"

"Precisely."

"You landed Garret Harley's account. Congratulations. And now, guess what?"

Kaitlin leaned against the kitchen counter. "I don't know, but don't tell me you're getting married."

There was silence on the other end.

"Barbara?"

Then she heard her cousin inhale and exhale. "But, Kaitlin," she said, and her voice sounded hurt, "I *am* getting married." Then all the tremendous excitement returned. "Kaitlin, believe it or not—finally!— he wants to get married. I thought you'd be ecstatic for me. I know you've been with me through thick and thin on this one. Kaitlin—"

"Wait, wait, wait!" Kaitlin said. "You're serious? Joe proposed?"

"Proposed, put a diamond on my finger and even got us a church date."

"Oh, Barbara! That's wonderful. I really am happy for you! It's just such a—a surprise."

Barbara giggled. "I guess it is. After the week you've already been having."

"You heard about Gram?"

"I have."

"She called you already?"

"No, Donna called me already. So I know about Gram. And Donna. And Donna knows about me. And I know that you're going to be her maid of honor, but I want you to be mine, too. You *should* be mine, actually. I mean, we live so close, it seems we spend half our lives together."

"I'd—I'd love to be your maid of honor, too. When is the wedding?"

The pang, the stupid little nasty pang, struck her again. Hard, this time. Like a knife right to the heart. She clenched her teeth and ignored it. No one deserved this kind of happiness more than Barbara. It was just that Joe and Brendan were friends, and thinking of one man made her think of the other, too.

The past seemed to be crashing down upon her.

Go away! she screamed in silence. Then the pain faded, and she was truly happy, happy for Barbara.

She listened to Barbara, trying to think. If Donna's wedding was in October and Barbara's was in November, it could work. She would just have to do a lot of running back and forth, but she loved them both. How could she turn down either one of them?

And then there was her grandmother...but that would be over very soon. While she was listening, she scratched a note on her wall calendar to buy something nice for dinner that weekend. If Gram loved this nice Mr. Rosen, than Kaitlin was going to do her best to make him happy, comfortable and well-fed.

"Well?" Barbara prompted.

"Everything sounds fine," Kaitlin told her. "Oh, Barbara! Finally! After all this time! And he really wants a big wedding, the whole works?"

"He said that he'd do it however I wanted to do it." She laughed suddenly. "Don't forget—my parents still think I'm living with you."

Kaitlin was certain that Barbara's parents didn't really think so—they just wanted to—but she couldn't see any reason to remind Barbara of that now, when she was about to become legally wed—and totally legitimate.

"There's more to tell you," Barbara said. Then she was suddenly in a rush. "But I'll have to call back.

Just promise me that you'll do it. You won't back out if things get a little sticky?''

"Sticky? What should get sticky?" Kaitlin asked.

"I'll explain later. But if you can handle it for Donna, then you can handle it for me."

"Handle it? What—"

"Oh! Donna didn't tell you? We're sharing more than a maid of honor. I can't get into it now, though. Just promise me you'll do it. Be my maid of honor. Promise me! I just realized I'm late as heck for work, and I'm not my own boss. I'll get back to you as soon as I can."

"Fine," Kaitlin said. "I promise." Then she hung up and stared out the window. "Damn!" she whispered aloud. "It *must* be something in the water."

She did make it to work by late afternoon. As she strolled through the attractive outer office she paused by Sam's desk. "Screen my relatives for me, will you, Sam?"

"Your family?" Sam said, amazed.

Kaitlin nodded dryly. "If they're calling to ask me to be in a wedding, tell them I've disappeared. Even if they're only calling to ask me *to* a wedding, you can still tell them I've disappeared." She walked into her office and managed to get some scheduling done. She reached the director she wanted for the Seashell commercial, and she got Sally from the agency to verify that she had the actor and actress Kaitlin wanted.

That night she tried to reach Barbara, but all she got was the answering machine. She left Joe her congratulations and Barbara a message to get back to her. Knowing that she would be at the beach shooting all the next day, she left the resort's phone number.

The day of the commercial dawned beautifully.

Kaitlin arrived at Addison's Resort, on the Key, to find that her director and her actors had already arrived. Netty was in the coffee shop, and Janis drove up just as she did, bringing the swimsuits, the accessories and, of course, the product, Seashell Sunblock.

Kaitlin met Janis in the suite she had rented for the shoot and smiled. "So far, so good," she told her, then ran through her checklist again. Danny was on his way to set up the scene. He should arrive by the time Mark and Cissy were dressed and ready to go.

"Let's leave the suite to Mark and Cissy. We'll start with the beach scene. We'll meet Lenny down by the pool and grab some coffee ourselves. How does that sound?"

"Great," Janis said. "Why do I feel so jittery? As if something's bound to go wrong?"

"Nothing is going to go wrong," Kaitlin assured her. She herself felt great. Things seemed to be moving perfectly.

Lenny was already downstairs at one of the huge umbrella tables by the pool overlooking the beautiful white sands of the private beach. He pointed out his cameramen by the water, busily checking light levels and their equipment.

"I just hope we finish today," Lenny told her. He was thirty-three, blond and balding, and possessed of a definitely artistic temperament, but he was quick to laugh at himself and able to work well with Kaitlin's ideas. She used him as often as she was able to get him.

"Why shouldn't we?" she asked him with a frown. The wind was picking up by the water. She was wearing sunglasses, a big, droopy straw hat and a candy-striped sleeveless dress cinched at the waist with a wide red belt. It had been a mistake. Even as she sat at the table, the wind whipped at her skirt.

"Mark is having some problems."

With his lover? Kaitlin wondered. Mark Ford was a gorgeous male. Tall, dark, extremely hunky. He was also gay, but he was usually dependable and wonderful to work with. Kaitlin had chosen him very carefully. She liked him a lot, knew he liked her, and couldn't believe that he would jeopardize such an important job.

"It's been touch and go with one of his favorite aunts," Lenny told her. "Cancer. He was just on the phone in the hallway."

"Oh," she said softly. "I'm sorry." She *was* sorry. And she hoped that God would forgive her if she prayed that Mark's aunt stayed alive until after the shoot.

She realized how horrible she was being and told herself that they would just have to reschedule. Even as she did so, the waiter came up, and handed her the phone. "Call for you, Ms. O'Herlihy."

Kaitlin thanked him and picked up the receiver. It was Barbara.

"Barbara!" She had wanted to talk to her cousin so badly, and she had thought that she'd have plenty of time, waiting around the set.

"I'll check on things. I see Cissy coming," Lenny whispered to her.

"Thanks!" she said and watched him walk toward the model. "Barbara, I may have to get back to you—" she began. Then she noticed that Cissy was pouting at something Lenny said. The model stamped a foot.

"Kaitlin? You okay? Got a second? I just wanted to get back to you about what I was saying the other night."

"Yes, yes, of course. This mystery thing," she murmured. What was going on? Cissy was shouting about something.

Cissy, unlike Mark, was not easy to work with. She was stunningly beautiful, and she knew it. She thought that she should have been discovered for big-time movies by now.

Barbara was saying something. Kaitlin, watching the exchange between Cissy and Lenny, wasn't really listening.

"We share the same best man, too."

"Really?" Kaitlin murmured politely.

"And I don't want you to be upset."

"No, no, of course not." Upset? She was about to get hysterical. Cissy had just hauled off and given Lenny a big slap, then spun around and walked away.

"Oh, hell and damnation!" Kaitlin muttered. "Barb, I'll have to call you back."

"Right! Just let me tell you who it is—"

Lenny, enraged, was back. "Cissy says she isn't coming back. Mark is gone—he headed for New York. Cissy said he had no right to go. That she doesn't give a damn about Mark or his aunt. She won't work again in this town, not for me. I swear it, Kaitlin—if you're going to work with her again, don't call me."

She vaguely heard Lenny, and she vaguely heard Barbara.

Vaguely. Just vaguely. Because her jaw had dropped and her ears were buzzing, and it seemed that the world was spinning.

There was a man coming toward her. A tall, dark-haired man in bathing trunks. A tall, beautifully bronzed man with wonderfully rugged features and startling green eyes with golden-fire specks.

Brendan.

She knew he had a home here. She knew he kept boats here. She'd read bits and pieces about him in the papers over the years. And she'd even seen him, in the Keys. Not so long ago. Not long enough ago.

But they hadn't met face to face, not here, and she hadn't imagined that they ever would. There were three million people in Dade and Broward counties.

But in the midst of all this, Brendan was coming toward her.

"Barbara, I really have to hang up now," she said to the receiver.

"Wait!" Barbara shrieked. "I have to tell you. He wants to talk to you. He took a room at the hotel, and I'm sure he's going to look you up today."

"He? Barbara, what are you talking about?"

Closer. He was coming closer. And suddenly she didn't feel a day over eighteen. If she had been standing, she would have fallen.

There was hair on his chest. Rich, dark hair. Very masculine. A gold St. Christopher's medal dangled there, somehow adding to the appeal. He'd aged. Some. There was just a touch of silver at his temples.

"He?" she whispered sickly.

"Brendan, Kaitlin. Brendan is our best man. And he's going to be Bill's best man, too. Anyway, he wanted Bill and Donna to ask you first, but when Joe approached him, well, he said he had to talk to you himself. That you're a relative and he's just a good friend, and that he's willing as long as you don't feel there would be any problem. And, well, I wanted time to talk to you, but you know Brendan, he said he had to know for himself that it was okay—Kaitlin, are you there?"

She was there. But Netty was suddenly there, too, staring at Brendan and smiling. Actually smiling.

"Oh, Ms. O'Herlihy, he *is* perfect! Definitely perfect!"

"But that's not Mark Ford!" Janis whispered anxiously.

"Kaitlin, are you there?" Barbara demanded.

By then Brendan was there, right there in front of her.

Smooth and muscled and sleek—and half naked. He seemed to dwarf everything else. And he was talking softly, his voice low and rich and resonant.

"Kaitlin, I'm sorry to interrupt you—excuse me, really—but I just wanted to see if we could meet later. Barbara promised that she would have explained things to you by now and—"

"Perfect!" Netty cried again, clapping her hands together. And then she put her arms on his shoulders and turned him to face her.

She actually put her hands on him—on Brendan!—and dragged him around.

Kaitlin saw his muscles tighten, saw his jaw go tense. He might have grown lots more hair on his chest, but it didn't seem that his temper had changed a bit.

"Wait!" she shrieked, leaping to her feet. The phone fell to the tiled floor. She could vaguely hear Barbara's voice, and she wished that Barbara was there at that moment, because she wanted to throttle her cousin into silence.

"Mrs. Green, this isn't my model. There's been quite a mix-up, I'm afraid—"

"Nonsense!" Netty insisted. "He's perfect."

Brendan's temper seemed to have faded. He was confused, he was irritated, but he wasn't going to do anything incredibly rude. "Perfect?" he inquired politely. "Well, thank you. But I don't think that Ms. O'Herlihy would agree with you." ·

"Oh, Kaitlin, come on! Seashell Sunblock is my product, and I think he's perfect."

"But he's not a model!" Kaitlin insisted.

"No, he's not," Brendan agreed, and his voice was very firm. "Kaitlin, if you can manage a few minutes later, I'll be down by the water." He stared at Netty Green. "Excuse me, ma'am, it's been a pleasure."

"Oh, wait! Wait!" Netty cried. "If you're not the model, just who are you?"

He paused, his back stiffening. Then he turned slowly, and the way his eyes fell on Kaitlin, she suddenly felt as if no time at all had passed since their last meeting.

As if dreams had never shattered between them.

Then his gaze was suddenly very cold and distant, and the smile he offered Netty was wry and amused. "I'm Mr. O'Herlihy. Brendan O'Herlihy, Miss . . . ?"

"Green," Netty said quickly. "Netty Green."

"Yes, well, nice to have met you, Miss Green." Then he turned again, and his muscles rippled in the sunlight as he started to walk away.

Janis, working on delayed reaction, gasped and leaped to her feet, staring after Brendan. It seemed as if her jaw was about to hit the floor. "That's him? Your ex?" she breathed incredulously.

Kaitlin fell into her chair. She couldn't answer.

She didn't need to. Brendan paused and turned slowly. "Yes," he said, his gaze sweeping over the table. "I'm him. Her ex." His eyes landed on Kaitlin one last time and swept over her curiously; then he was walking away.

Yes, it was very definitely Brendan. But he wasn't walking away, not really.

On the contrary, she thought, trembling. He had just walked back into her life.

Chapter 2

That man is perfect!" Netty Green repeated obstinately.

Kaitlin, staring after Brendan's retreating back, clenched her teeth tightly to keep from replying too quickly. She even managed to smile past the grid lock of her teeth. Then, after a few deep breaths, she managed to speak with an even tone and a surprising amount of polite control.

"Netty, I really am sorry, but I can't make a man be a model who does not choose to be a model. And despite our very best efforts, I am afraid that I'm going to have to reschedule."

Netty set her thin little lips and raised her chin. "Ms. O'Herlihy, I am not willing to reschedule. My time is valuable. I'm afraid I can give you only thirty minutes to solve this dilemma, and that is that."

She turned, her narrow back ramrod straight, and disappeared into the hotel.

Kaitlin allowed her hand to crash straight down on the table, groaning. "Where did I go wrong? It was college, I know it. I should have gone to medical school. Gram always wanted someone in the family to be a doctor."

"Kaitlin!" Janis said, her voice low but edged with a trace of excitement. "This is still salvageable."

"Don't mention salvage. It's part of what he does for a living."

"Your ex?"

"Don't call him that."

"Okay. Mr. O'Herlihy?"

Kaitlin nodded bleakly, her head still on the table.

"Well, that doesn't matter," Janis said. "Listen to me now! Pay attention. He came here to see you. He wants peace between you. He's offering an olive branch—"

"If he's offering it, it's a barbed olive branch, believe me," Kaitlin moaned, but she managed to sit up.

"Kaitlin, how bad can this be? You've been apart a long time now—"

"No, no, not so long." All right, it was a long time. Eight years since they were divorced. But she had seen him less than four years ago, when she'd asked him if they couldn't seek an annulment to appease both sets of very Catholic parents.

She hadn't gotten an annulment. What she *had* gotten had been enough to make her very, very careful now.

"Kaitlin, you've got to ask him to model for this commercial."

"No!"

"Kaitlin, what is your problem? He seems mature and pleasant, and he's one of the most handsome, masculine men I've ever seen. He *is* perfect! A wonderful model—"

"He doesn't want to be a model."

"Tell him that it's acting."

"Janis, I can't!" she insisted.

"You have to! We're going to lose this account if you don't."

"We don't have a female model anymore," Kaitlin reminded her.

"We'll get one. Just go get that man!"

"Janis, so we lose the account . . ."

"And then I don't get paid!" Janis wailed. "Kaitlin, this is important. We could keep Seashell Products for years and years. Please!"

"Janis—"

"He wants something from you, right? So go out there and get something from him!"

"I need a drink," Kaitlin muttered.

"It's first thing in the morning!"

"Irish whiskey, neat."

"Go get him, Kaitlin. Think of our reputation. Think of the business."

"I'm thinking about my sanity," Kaitlin said wearily. She sipped at her cold coffee. It was fine. Anything to wet her parched throat.

What had she done that was so evil that it seemed God was punishing her with a day like today?

If she found that Gram had included Brendan in her wedding, too, well, then, Kaitlin would probably just explode in shock and that would be that. All over.

"Kaitlin!" Janis wailed. "We're running out of time."

Kaitlin stood. Janis was right. Kaitlin needed to salvage something out of this situation. It was just that it was so dangerous to go near him. She should know. After what happened when she had seen him about the annulment...

Because things didn't change. Things never changed between them. Emotions always roiled just beneath the surface. Anger, pain, even laughter, and that deeplying thing had made it possible for time to erase anything between them.

But she was going to have to see him anyway. There was no way out of it. She couldn't possibly tell her cousins she wouldn't be involved in their weddings if Brendan were involved, too. She just couldn't.

"Go get him, tiger!" Janis applauded.

"Janis!"

"Well...?"

Kaitlin inhaled and started walking down the beach. She passed Lenny's cameraman with all his equipment and smiled, as if nothing in the world was wrong. "Are we still on, Ms. O'Herlihy?" he called to her.

"I—maybe," she answered. She could see Brendan again. He was a little further down the beach, seated in the sand, his elbows on his knees, a blade of beach grass in his mouth as he stared out to sea. A trembling began deep within her abdomen. What had gone so wrong between them? Had it been because they looked at life with the eyes of youth, expectant, hopeful, believing in ideals?

And then life had been so cruel. Even so, when she had seen him several years ago they had still managed to laugh. Then the laughter had died away, and they had discovered that other things remained, the passion remained....

He turned, as if he had sensed her. She kept walking, despite the lump in her throat. Then the wind picked up, and suddenly her candy-striped skirt was swirling around her thighs.

She swore, pressing it down. He was wearing his sunglasses, but she saw the smile that curved his lips and she knew he was aware of her discomfort.

She held the skirt at her side and anchored her hat with her other hand before the wind could whip it away, too.

It got harder as she got closer, but she kept walking, and within moments, she was standing before him.

"Hi," he said, and patted the sand. "Take a seat."

She bit into her bottom lip, but sat beside him. For a moment she, too, stared out to sea.

"I take it that Barbara hadn't told you anything?" he finally asked, turning to her.

She could feel his green gaze despite his dark glasses. She didn't look at him. She wished that she hadn't sat quite so close. He had showered recently and he smelled nicely of soap mingled with his own scent, and with the salty smell of the sea.

He *was* perfect.

His bare shoulders were bronzed, strong. He had gotten more attractive with age, she thought. His chest was so broad, so nicely muscled.

And so damn bare.

Even if she hadn't know him before, she would have been tempted to touch. To explore that rich, dark flurry of hair that grew over the rippling muscles...

"Kaitlin?"

"Ah...yes, Barbara did talk to me. About five minutes ago. Right while you were walking up to the table," she managed to say.

"No warning? I'm sorry."

She shrugged. "Well, you know Barbara."

"And Joe," he agreed, and though he was looking out to sea once again, she could see his easy smile from the corner of her eye. "Can you believe that they're finally getting married?" He chuckled softly.

"Yes, I can," she said with a trace of indignation in her tone. She added, "I still believe in magic," then regretted the words. They gave away so much.

He glanced at her and shrugged. "Yes, well, maybe it is out there," he said softly. Then he went quickly to the point. "Do you mind?"

"That they're getting married? Of course not. I think it's wonderful."

"No," Brendan groaned. "I meant, do you mind that I'm going to be involved in these weddings, too? Because if it's going to bother you at all, I'll step aside."

She lowered her head, staring at the sand. "It's really none of my business. Bill has a right to his choice, and so does Joe. And if they both want you—"

"Kaitlin, I asked if *you* minded."

"And I said—"

"Kaitlin?"

"Well, of course I mind!" she exploded, and she was instantly on her feet, in all of five minutes he'd managed to completely destroy her well-earned, customary control. "Of course I mind, but—"

"Kaitlin, I said that I—"

"No! No! You're going to be Bill's best man, and you're going to be Joe's best man. You just can't have my blessing, that's all. I don't think I can be cheerful and smile every time I see you."

"Then—"

"But I *will* see you. And we *will* get through it."

He was smiling, she realized. And he was barely listening to her.

"Your skirt, Kaitlin. It's better than Marilyn Monroe on that subway grating."

She gasped and collected her flying skirt. Afterward she felt his hand on her wrist, pulling her down beside him. "Funny, isn't it? I don't have a right in the world where you're concerned, Ms. O'Herlihy, but though I'm impressed as hell by that sexy red garter and those sleek stockings, I still can't handle the thought of another man enjoying the show."

"Brendan—"

"I won't seduce you, Kaitlin."

"Oh, God!" she whispered, mortified, trying to jerk her wrist from his grasp.

"The last time I saw you, I really couldn't help it. You wanted something from me. You wanted to pretend that we had never been married. After you'd spent all these years using my name. And you still wanted the name! You wanted the annulment, too. And it seemed as if you were willing to pay anything to get what you wanted. I really couldn't help myself."

"Brendan, let go of my wrist!" she whispered, then swung on him when he didn't let go. "Your ego is incredible. I couldn't have been seduced—especially by you—if I hadn't let it happen. So don't assume that you can crook a finger and have me come running."

"I never assumed that, Kaitlin," he said coldly. "There were times when I could have begged and it wouldn't have brought you near me."

She gasped, and suddenly her lips were trembling. She was so filled with emotion that she was shaking all over. "You left, Brendan O'Herlihy! You left me right after our wedding—or what sufficed for a wedding! And then you left the country. Even before that you left me. You left me when Sean died. You were gone even when you were standing right beside me."

"For God's sake, Kaitlin—"

"It still hurts, doesn't it? It still hurts that Sean died. Well, what happened between us still hurts, too."

She shut up suddenly, aware that her eyes were watering, aware that she had said things she had never intended to say. It was just that, when he was with her, time and distance disappeared. It had been the same when she had gone to see him before. When they had begun to talk. But she had been casual then. She had tried to pretend that time had taken away all the pain, all the longing. She had been mature and distant as she explained what she wanted and why it would be best for them both.

He had listened. Then he had moved closer, and she had felt all the same things that seeing him now was making her feel again. The urge to stroke his cheek, to run her fingers over his back, over his bronzed flesh. They'd been sipping wine, and he'd been listening so seriously to everything she'd had to say....

She couldn't regret it. Not what had happened between them. But she had been furious about the morning after. About his blunt reminder that she'd been using his name all these years, and that they *had* been married, and that he would never say any different. And then he'd been quick to leave, inviting her to come back whenever she wanted to see him, just see him, without expecting anything else.

She hadn't gone back. She'd felt like a fool. And now...

"Does it still hurt?" he asked her softly.

"Yes," she replied honestly. "Not every day." She smiled. "In fact, I pride myself on the fact that endless days can go by during which I don't think about you once. But yes, it's there, in a corner of my heart."

"Is it?" he asked very quietly, but then she realized that he was looking beyond her shoulder and frowning. He smiled at her, arching a brow. "Your friend is hopping up and down and waving wildly. And tapping her wristwatch."

"Oh!" Kaitlin gasped, startled. She stared at the sand miserably. She couldn't ask him. He had told her once not to come back unless she came because she wanted him—and not something from him. But he'd made such a fool of her, hurt her so badly, that she'd never been able to go back. And now...

"She seems to want you," Brendan observed.

"Yes," Kaitlin said. She turned so she could see Janis hopping up and down, too. She waved reassuringly and stared at the sand again.

"If you need to get to work..." Brendan began.

"I don't. Not really. The shoot fell apart and Netty Green is pulling the spot."

"Why?" he demanded sharply.

She gazed at him. "She wants you."

"Who wants me? For what?" he asked, annoyed.

Kaitlin exhaled and scrambled to her feet. She stared at him without answering, holding her skirt at her thigh. "Brendan, I wouldn't hurt my cousins or ruin their weddings for anything. We can get along for the little time we need to be together, I'm sure of it."

He had a very skeptical look on his face as he got to his feet. "Sure," he said briefly. Then he caught her hand. She felt his fingers moving against her palm, and she wanted to scream. "Now, tell me, what's going on with your shoot?"

"It isn't your problem, Brendan."

"Tell me."

"No."

"Why not?"

"Because it isn't any of your business. Because..." She hesitated.

"Go on."

"Because you told me not to ask you for anything again."

He stiffened. "Oh. So you did walk down the beach to ask me for something."

"Yes. No! I walked down the beach because I had to talk to you. Because we had to straighten this out. And because—"

"Because what?" he snapped. She had forgotten that his hold could be so steely, that his fingers could clamp around her wrist like a vice.

"You heard her!" Kaitlin snapped. "She wants you to be her model."

"I've never modeled in my life! I race boats and I dive for wrecks."

"I know, Brendan, but—"

"You mean that woman is going to pull the entire campaign if she doesn't get me in her commercial?" he asked incredulously.

"Yes. She—she thinks you're perfect," Kaitlin replied irritably.

He was grinning as he released her suddenly. "Well," he murmured, stroking his chin.

"I'm not asking you to do it, Brendan. I can't afford your price."

His grin faded. She could read nothing of his thoughts from his features, and his dark glasses shadowed his eyes. "I told you I wouldn't seduce you again, Kaitlin," he said harshly. "If that's what you're afraid of."

"I'm not afraid of you, Brendan. I told you, it was as much my fault as yours."

"How interesting. And magnanimous."

"It's nothing."

"We're going to be seeing each other a number of times," he reminded her.

"Yes, we've established that—"

"And I won't stop you if you try to seduce me," he said softly. Huskily. His words seemed to hang on the breeze. To linger. To reach out and touch her more surely than any caress.

"That should hardly worry either of us," she murmured coolly.

"We'll see. What happened to your model?" he asked suddenly, changing the subject.

"What?"

"Your model. Why does your lady need a male body to begin with?"

"Oh." He had changed from her personal life to her professional life too quickly. She shrugged. "An illness in the family. And it doesn't matter. I lost my female model, too. I—"

"All right," he said suddenly.

"All right what?" she asked nervously.

"All right, I'll do it."

"You'll do what?"

"I'll model for your commercial. You're supposed to be talking me into it, right? That's why your friend keeps hopping around and tapping her watch. I'll do it. On one condition."

"And what's that?" Kaitlin asked softly, suspiciously.

He was quiet for a minute, watching her. The sun beat down on them, and she found herself studying him, seeing the man she had known forever, but also seeing the stranger he had become. The little touches of silver at his temples added to his mystique. The dark glasses shadowed his eyes, kept him from revealing any truths. The set of his jaw was as square as ever; his shoulders were as taut and broad and square as they had always been.

One condition . . .

Maybe he would ask for one last night. One last chance to be together, to believe in magic. To forget time and eternity and the world, and bask in the moonlight and the night air. To feel the caress of the breeze, and of one another. To soar and savor flesh and blood and passion.

Her cheeks colored, and she lowered her lashes, fearful that her eyes would betray her thoughts. She knotted her fingers into fists and held them behind her. The desire to touch him was suddenly so strong she could hardly resist. To touch, to stroke. To follow the thin dark line where the mat of chest hair narrowed provocatively at his waistband. To step closer and press her lips against his, to feel the hunger of his kiss . . .

"One condition," he repeated.

"Yes?" Her lashes were falling, closing over her eyes. Let it be decadent, let it be crude! She could protest, of course, and be indignant, but then . . .

"You have to model, too."

Her eyes flew open. "What?"

"Well, if I'm going to spend the day being a piece of meat, you can join me. I'll model—if you will."

Her secret desires came spiraling through her with shocking clarity, and she stared at him incredulously. He didn't want to go to bed with her. He didn't want one last night together.

Not even an hour.

He just wanted to make sure she didn't get anything for free.

She shook her head, backing away, feeling like a fool—and wishing she could dunk him in the ocean.

"I can't. It's out of the question."

"Why not? Gained too much weight in the thighs?"

"No!"

"Well, then?"

"I'm not a model!"

"And neither am I. But I'm willing to give it a fling to save your business. Why aren't you?"

"My whole business will not fall apart if I do not keep this account!"

"Ah, but it will be injured," he said smugly.

"How can you be so sure?"

"Because of that person up there, hopping away like a pogo stick."

"Oh!" She spun to see that Janis was desperately trying to get her attention. And Netty Green was walking toward the table. It was now or never.

The Seashell Sunblock account *was* important. No, she wouldn't lose her business, but . . .

Other clients would know that Seashell had pulled out. They would wonder why, and few people would stop to realize that Netty Green was a pain in the . . .

"Hey, kid, this one is up to you," Brendan reminded her softly.

She spun to face him. "All right, all right!"

"Don't jump down my throat. It's your business, not mine."

"That's right. You make a living out of being a pirate."

"A pirate?" His brows shot up. "Because I search for ships that sank hundreds of years ago?" He wasn't really expecting an answer. "There's more, too," he told her.

"What do you mean, there's more?" she asked suspiciously. A little dance of heat was already taking place all along her spine.

"Dinner."

"What dinner?"

"Any dinner. You and I alone. Just to discuss the basics—"

"What damn basics?"

His brows shot up in surprise, and he smiled then, very slowly. "The weddings, Kaitlin. Some of the things I know Donna and Bill and Barbara and Joe would like. What I think we should do for them."

"What you think...!"

"Kaitlin, damn it, I want your opinion, too. That's why I'd like to go to dinner. A *friendly* dinner. To discuss things. Look, these ladies are your cousins, and I said I would step aside—"

"No! I told you I don't want that."

He was silent for a moment. As she watched him, she wondered why he couldn't have lost every hair on his head.

No...he probably would have been attractive bald, too. He'd need to lose his whole damn head. Turn pink. Cease to smile, to speak...

And he wanted dinner.

"Kaitlin, I know you wish I'd disappear from these weddings—actually, I imagine you wish I'd disappear from the face of the earth. But you don't want to be responsible for my absence."

She smiled sweetly. "Brendan, you're wrong. I hope you live forever."

"Just nowhere near you, right?"

She shrugged, and he laughed. Then his smile faded, and he demanded abruptly, "Have we got a deal?"

"What?"

"A deal, Kaitlin. I model if you model, and then I get dinner. The weekend after next. I'm working this weekend, and this *is* supposed to be at my convenience."

"But if I model—"

"It's your business, remember?"

The weekend after next was Gram's wedding.

"Wednesday. I don't have a weekend night free."

"I'll get you at eight."

Still, she hesitated. Dinner. With Brendan. Alone. Well, he wasn't going to seduce her. Did she trust him?

Damn. Did she trust herself? Twice burned . . .

He pointed toward the hotel once again. "Your friend is getting very nervous."

"Yes!"

"You'll model and join me for dinner?"

"All right, all right. I'll model, and—and go to dinner. And I won't renege."

"Fine," he said flatly.

Janis was slamming her fingers against her watch. Netty would be walking away any second.

"Okay, Brendan, come on, then," Kaitlin muttered, turning. "Please, let's just do this and get it over with."

"Gee, when you phrase things so charmingly, it really is hard to resist," he mocked.

What was the matter with her? He could still back out of the deal.

But he was behind her. "It won't be quite over with," he reminded her.

"Right. Dinner," she said.

He laughed huskily, but he was with her. And that was important. He was behind her all the way past the cameraman and the equipment and to the table, where Netty Green was beaming.

"Oh, I am so pleased, Mr. O'Herlihy. I do understand that this is not your vocation, and I thank you sincerely. I promise you that my product is a very good one."

"I know your product, Mrs. Green," Brendan began.

Terrified of what he might say, Kaitlin jumped in quickly. "Is Lenny close by, Janis?"

Janis nodded, her eyes darting from Kaitlin to Brendan, and started to speak. "Yes, he's in the suite, waiting. He said—"

"Well, Mr. O'Herlihy, what do you think of Seashell Sunblock?" Netty demanded.

Kaitlin held her breath. Brendan was going to tell the truth—no matter what it was.

"It's a good product. It compares with the established brands, and the price is low enough for the young mother with a bunch of kids to stock up on it. I wouldn't have agreed to this—no matter what—if I had been asked to sell something I couldn't truly endorse."

Netty was beaming, absolutely beaming. Kaitlin didn't think she could take any more of it. "Did Cissy leave the suit, do you know?" she asked Janis.

Janis stared at her blankly for a moment. "Oh, yes, yes, she did. But I haven't called for another model, because I didn't know—"

"It doesn't matter. I'm going to do it," Kaitlin said.

"You're going to call?"

"No, I'm going to be the model."

Janis dropped her jaw, Netty cocked her head, and Kaitlin could feel the smile on Brendan's face.

"You're—you're going to be the model?" Janis said.

"Yes!" Kaitlin snapped. Then she spun around. "I'll go change. I'll be right down. I'll send Lenny to the beach, and you alert the cameraman." Janis had yet to close her mouth. She kept looking from Brendan to Kaitlin, who ignored her.

"Brendan, Lenny may want to put some pancake makeup on your face. I know that—"

"Fine."

He wasn't going to fight with her. He was still wearing the glasses, but his features were calm and composed, and he was being completely charming, the easiest man in the world with whom to get along.

She wanted to hit him.

Instead, she smiled. "Well, then, I'll go change."

She swung around and hurried up to the suite. Lenny was sitting on the sofa, watching a talk show. He looked up, surprised, as she breezed in. "Are we on or off?"

"On!" Kaitlin snapped, marching by him and heading for the bedroom. The two-piece bathing suit was on the bed, and there was an array of makeup spread out on the dresser.

"Glad to hear you so pleased and excited!" Lenny called to her.

She slammed the door. In seconds she had stripped, throwing her clothes wherever they landed, and donned the suit. She sat before the mirror, darkening her eyes carefully and doing her face. There was a knock on the door.

"Hey, Kaitlin! What's up?" It was Lenny.

"Come on in," she called to him.

He opened the door and stared at her, then began to smile. "So..."

"Don't 'so' me."

"I think you're perfect."

She groaned softly. "And don't use that word, please!"

"Okay, you'll stink, but what the hell."

"Lenny..."

"Seriously, I think you'll be great. I think it's a major loss that you never put yourself in front of the camera before."

"Lenny, how's the makeup?"

He came over and studied her closely. "Seems perfect—sorry, seems fine. Where's Mr. Perfect—whoops! Sorry, can't seem to shake that word."

"Manage it, huh?" Kaitlin murmured.

He grinned.

"Why doesn't anyone take my temper seriously?" she moaned.

"An Irish temper? I take it very seriously, Kaitlin, me love," he teased. "I'll go down and check out your man."

"He's not my man."

"He is today," Lenny advised her. He closed the door, and Kaitlin closed her eyes, then opened them and studied her face once again. Maybe she would be all right. The makeup made her eyes huge, and, if nothing else, her hair had color and luster. It was probably too long, but she wasn't going to go around chopping off her hair for a sixty-second commercial.

Sixty seconds...that would take them hours. Hours and hours of putting sunblock on Brendan or—worse—feeling him put it on her.

She groaned and leaned her head against her arms. Well, she was committed. She might as well face the music.

She stood and hurried out of the room to the elevator. Then she realized she had brought nothing with her, no shoes, no towel, no cover-up. And there was a slightly balding man in the elevator with her. Leering. She felt naked. She *was* half naked. Anyone in her right mind would have grabbed a cover-up.

She wasn't in her right mind.

When the elevator stopped, she nearly ran to the table. Janis was waiting for her; the others were already down on the beach.

"You look like dynamite!" Janis assured her. "But how—"

"Don't ask."

"You'll be just per—"

"Don't! Don't say it! Let's just go, okay?"

Janis studied her and nodded, grinning from ear to ear despite her best efforts. "All right, you look like pure garbage. Is that better?"

"No!"

"I wouldn't be so grouchy if I was the one putting lotion on him," Janis commented.

"You weren't married to him."

"No," Janis said with a sigh. "I wouldn't have let him go."

"I didn't—oh, never mind. Please, let's just get this over with!"

It wasn't going to be that easy; she had been sure of that, and she'd been right.

Lenny had worked on Brendan, who was wearing makeup on his nose and cheeks and shoulders. His sunglasses were gone, and his eyes were a startling deep green against his bronze flesh, his dark hair a perfect frame for his face. He watched Kaitlin approach, and his gaze swept slowly over her. He smiled, but she wasn't sure whether it was because she hadn't changed—or because she had. She was about to speak when Netty came rushing forward.

"I knew it, I knew it! It's exactly the look I want. Older, sophisticated—well, not too old, of course, but—oh, Kaitlin, I am so pleased and eager to see the final product!"

"We should get to it," Lenny advised. "Morning light, you know."

"Sure," Kaitlin murmured.

There was a huge towel stretched out on the beach in front of the cameras, and a large bottle of Seashell Sunblock was waiting on it. An ice chest sat on one corner of the blanket; sandals and a couple of paperbacks were strewn on another. It was an average day at the beach.

"Kaitlin, Brendan, remember, there's going to be a voice-over. Don't worry about sound. The surf and breeze will be added to the mix later. Action is all that we need. Is that all right, Brendan? Do you understand?"

"I think I've got the basics," Brendan said dryly.

"Great."

"Brendan, the voice-over is saying, 'When you touch her this afternoon, touch her with Seashell Sunblock'—then the scene will switch. Janis will read the line. And what I want is Kaitlin on her knees, and you right behind her. Make use of her hair. Sweep it aside to get the lotion on her nape and along her back and shoulders. Okay? Kaitlin, down on your knees."

She went down. This was her commercial. She had written it. She hadn't planned on being the one on her knees . . . with Brendan behind her.

Touching her.

"Okay, Janis, give Brendan the line. Slowly."

So Janis read.

And Brendan touched.

He swept her hair aside, and his fingers moved smoothly over her skin. Slick, fragrant with the lotion. Warm, soothing, rippling along her shoulders and spine, touching her flesh, massaging her, moving down her back. She couldn't breathe. She could only feel him. His touch, his body, behind her. Close. His every breath touching her flesh where it was slick and smooth and cool with the lotion . . .

"Brendan, that's wonderful. Kaitlin, what the hell is the matter with you?"

"What?"

"That would have been it! A one-shot wrap. Kaitlin, this is your lover, your best friend in the world, the man you travel the globe with. Smile! You like him, remember? Loosen up! Glance his way over your shoulder. You like it! Got it?"

She gritted her teeth. "Got it."

"Okay, Jerry," Lenny called to the cameraman, checking the angle himself. "Action, please."

Janis began to read.

And Kaitlin found herself being bathed in lotion once again. She felt his fingertips. Felt the trembling they created deep down inside her. She moistened her lips and closed her eyes. She felt the sun, and she felt his touch. Stroking, his head bent close to hers. And she heard his barely breathed whisper. "Like it, Kaitlin?"

She didn't snap; she didn't break. She turned and smiled, just as she had been told, her eyes alive, her gaze as wicked as his fingertips. . . .

Lenny groaned. Kaitlin had been fine this time, but a kid running on the sand had caused the fly-up that the camera would surely catch. And then Netty suggested that when Brendan was done, he should give the lotion to Kaitlin, who could apply it to him as the shot faded away.

They went for seven takes in all.

On the last take, Kaitlin thought she would scream if she had to do it one more time. Had to feel his fingers moving against her flesh and muscle. Had to sense him behind her. Had to feel the strength and bulk of his body, smell his scent, feel the warmth of his breath caress her against the coolness of the lotion. Had to feel him stroking the length of her spine, stroking her shoulders, massaging her nape . . .

She was trembling when she turned. Smiled. Murmured a low, sultry thank you and took the lotion from his hands.

Then she touched him. All over his back. His broad, rippling, bronze and sexy back. She touched him from just above the buttocks, and swept upward, sheeting his back in lotion, and nearly touching him with the length of her body. Then he turned suddenly and her fingers were in the mat of hair on his chest and she was looking into his eyes. And her fingers were spreading the stuff outward, upward and downward, and she was still staring at him . . .

"Cut!" Lenny cried. And he jumped up and down. "That's a wrap. Perfect, damn, but that was perfect, Kaitlin, you can't imagine how perfect!"

His eyes were still on hers. It was over; people were moving. The cameraman was picking up his equipment, Lenny was hugging Janis, and Brendan was still staring at her with his magnetic green gaze. She couldn't seem to pull away from it. She was still trembling.

Then he smiled slowly. "Perfect," he said softly, turning as Netty came up to him.

Suddenly, on the beach, with the sun beating down on her, she was cold, shaking with it deep inside. Then Janis was behind her, whirling her around and whispering. "Dear Lord, I have never—never!—seen something so simple become so sensuous. I'm telling you, Kaitlin, this spot is mesmerizing. I could barely breathe right, just watching!"

"Janis! Please, stop!" Kaitlin said, her cheeks flaming. Just how sensuous had it appeared? And in front of all these people, too!

"But, Kaitlin, it *was* sexy. This product is going to walk off the shelves, I'm telling you. Just imagine—"

"Imagine what?" Kaitlin demanded.

"Why, we've just begun. Now he gets to carry you into the suite. Oh, it's wonderful that things didn't work out with Cissy and Mark! You two have such chemistry!"

Chemistry. Damn chemistry! Kaitlin thought. But Janis was right. It was there.

And they still had more to do.

Chapter 3

It was his fault. The whole damn thing was his fault, and Brendan knew it. He had never meant to say yes to her. And then, if he *was* going to agree to make an idiot of himself on camera, what had ever possessed him to demand that she join him, just so he could spend hour upon hour of torture, touching, stroking, caressing everything that he had vowed to himself— and to her—he wasn't going to have?

What a fool he had been.

Seashell Sunblock. Great. Wonderful. What on earth had gotten hold of him? After all these years, he should never be in such a position now.

Holding her. Dancing with her. Looking into her eyes, feeling the sway of her body, in the sweet heat of the night....

It had been bad enough at the beach. Touching her. Rubbing his fingers over her back, her shoulders. Sweeping her hair aside, inhaling her sweet scent. Touching her in front of all those people. Just how sensual could it have been?

Too sensual. The people had faded away, and he'd had trouble hearing. She had looked great in the blue two-piece bikini, tan, lean, compact, beautifully built.

Why couldn't she have gained about fifty pounds, accrued a few rotten teeth—or lost a whole mouthful of them—and maybe gone bald?

Then he wondered whether even those things would have changed anything.

He had wanted her all his life. Why should anything have changed?

They were off the beach now, and things were even worse. It was dark, and they were out on the patio. The moon was out, and they might have been alone, staring into one another's eyes. His fingers were curled around hers, his hand at the small of her back.

It shouldn't have felt so natural; it shouldn't have been so easy.

And he shouldn't have been waiting for so much of his life. He should have gotten married by now. He should have made damn sure he was at least seriously involved with someone so that she couldn't slip back into his life.

And she was in his life, all right. In his arms. In a strapless deep maroon cocktail dress with a skirt of some silky fabric that moved and swayed with every step. Her shoulder couldn't have been softer. They'd been bathed in sunblock all day long, and now her skin felt just like an angel's wings. And they were dancing close together. So close that he felt the tension rising in his body, so close that he felt every curve of her.

Curves he knew well. He could close his eyes, in fact, and summon up a memory of every curve and dip and nuance of her body. Colors and shapes and scents and essences, he could remember them all.

He had to quit remembering. It was embarrassing, because they weren't really alone.

There was a camera crew not ten feet away. And good old Lenny. And Janis, still rapt, still staring at him intently, still stuttering when she tried to talk to him. He liked her. She had an honesty that wouldn't allow her to pretend she'd never heard of him.

But exactly what had she heard? He didn't know.

And he couldn't begin to tell from looking into Kaitlin's eyes. Blue eyes. Wild, and anything but innocent. He would never forget the first time he'd seen her. She'd been flirting away, and the guys had all been panting after her like puppy dogs, just about tripping over their tongues. She had been defiant, challenging . . . and watching him in return. It had been fun at first, because he had known she was after him, making a bid for his attention.

And then she'd gotten it. He wasn't sure if it had been before or after he had taken her into his arms and danced with her—just like this—that he had realized he was interested, that he could never let her go.

He felt his jaw tightening. She was looking at him just as she had looked at him that night so long ago. With eyes that could melt steel. With a never-ending cascade of strawberry blond hair rippling down her back in lush waves of fire and gold.

He told himself that it was a commercial. A damn commercial and nothing else. There was no honesty in her eyes, none at all. It was over between them, all over, and it had been for a long time. She talked to him only when she wanted something from him.

Last time he'd made sure she hadn't gotten it. And this time . . .

Well, this time, they had to make peace. And they might have done it, if only he didn't have to touch her. If only he didn't feel just like a teenager—with *his* tongue on the floor this time.

No, it wasn't his tongue he was worried about.

He'd promised her he wouldn't seduce her, and she'd told him he didn't have the power. Not anymore. That he'd only been able to seduce her before because she had wanted him to.

Want me now, he thought. Want me.

Good, O'Herlihy, good, he told himself sarcastically. Let's start this whole thing off panting. It should make everything move right along.

It was just that when he held her like this, it was hard not to believe there was still something between them, no matter how much time had passed.

The last time he had held her this way had been almost four years ago, down in the Keys. The moon had been full and beautiful, and she had been in his arms, looking at him, her eyes very blue and very wide. He had been determined then that she wouldn't get away that night, that he would listen to her, that they would talk...

Then he had touched her, and when the music ended, he had carried her away...and refreshed his memory about her curves.

The scene felt so much the same now. No words between them, just the patio, the moonlight and Kaitlin in his arms. The only woman who both infuriated him and made him feel whole. He could lift her into his arms and sweep her away and— "Brendan! Wonderful!" Lenny called. The people in the background suddenly came crashing forward. "You two look wonderful. Janis is going to give you the line now. Just listen to it and keep up the good work. The camera is rolling."

Janis began to read huskily. "If you touch her this afternoon, touch her with Seashell Sunblock and be sure that you can touch her again tonight."

Kaitlin was still staring into his eyes. Her lips were soft, gleaming. She had never seemed more beautiful.

He wanted to shout, *It was my fault, damn it! When Sean died, the things that happened were my fault. I didn't stop loving you. It just seemed like everything else was so trivial. He'd been my best friend all my life, and he'd had so many hopes and plans and dreams, and suddenly they were all dead. I didn't know how to explain how I felt, how to cope with it. So I blocked you out, and then I lost you. I didn't even realize it until I saw you with another man. I thought it was my pride, but I really just didn't have the guts to admit that it was my fault, and I wanted to hurt you.*

"Okay, cut! That's a wrap!" Lenny was clapping his hands together.

Kaitlin dropped her hands and stepped away from him, a foot away. None of it had meant anything to her. It was just a commercial. A game. A tease.

Suddenly Lenny was there between the two of them, excited. "Kaitlin, I can't tell you how great the two of you look together!" He swung around to pump Brendan's hand. "You're wonderful. A natural. You should go into this for a living—"

"Oh, I've got a job, thank you. I'm a pirate," Brendan said, flashing a smile to Kaitlin, who didn't smile in return.

Lenny flashed Kaitlin a quick glance, then smiled at Brendan again. "We're almost finished here. We just need to go up to the hallway toward the suite. Pretend you're carrying your beloved off to bed. Think you can handle that as smoothly?"

Brendan met Kaitlin's eyes. "I can't wait," he said dryly.

She smiled sweetly. He could almost hear her teeth grating. "Oh, neither can I," she assured him.

"Okay!" Lenny called. "Let's wrap it up here and move upstairs, okay?"

Janis gathered up her papers, and the cameraman and his assistant began collecting their lights and equipment. Netty Green, who had been there all day, was still smiling. She placed a hand on Brendan's tuxedo-clad arm. "I must thank you again. You've been just what I wanted."

"Don't thank me, Mrs. Green," he said, his eyes still on Kaitlin. "Thank Kaitlin. She's always known how to get just what she wants."

"I just wish I knew how to repay you—" Netty began.

"Please, don't worry about it. Kaitlin pays very well. Very well, indeed."

Again he could almost hear the grating of her teeth. But she was still smiling. "He's a sucker for minimum wage, Netty. But it's nice to hear that you're so pleased." She turned to Brendan. "Thank you for working so hard. By the way, I think you need to fix your makeup. Your nose is shiny."

"My nose is shiny? Oh, no," he said with mock concern.

"It's the lights," she said sweetly. "They make us all perspire just a bit."

There went that tongue of hers as she moistened her lips again. She was shaken, as shaken as he was. If only there weren't so many people around.

"I think it's lovely that you two managed to part and remain such good friends!" Netty exclaimed, her thin fingers twining together, her eyes alight.

"Oh, yes, such friends," Kaitlin murmured. "Excuse me, Netty, will you? I'm going to run up and check a few things."

She was going to get away from him for a while, and they both knew it, Brendan thought. Maybe that was all right. He didn't seem to have a whole lot of control over his own reactions.

We never talked, he thought. And now, if I started talking, I wonder if she'd even remember what the problems were.

She was gone, and he gave himself a shake. "I guess it's going to take a few minutes for them to move all this stuff around, right?" he asked Netty.

She nodded, smiling and taking the arm he offered her.

"Can I buy you a drink, Mrs. Green?"

"Let me buy you one."

"No, thanks, I'm an old-fashioned guy at heart. What can I get you?"

She decided to have a glass of white wine. He sat with her at the bar and listened to her talk about her brother, and the growth of Seashell Products, and why it might seem that she was being petty, but all she really wanted was to protect her product. He half listened to her.

And he half ignored her, dreading, anticipating the moments to come.

He'd come here today to talk about arranging a special party for Barbara and Joe. Instead, he was in a tux, drinking Scotch in hopes that it would numb his fingers.

He hadn't seen her in almost four years, and it didn't matter, not one bit. It felt as if it had been yesterday. Maybe that was because he had seen too much of her when he *had* seen her.

He finished his drink. "I hear I need more makeup. I guess I'd better head up."

"Yes, yes, of course," Netty agreed.

They took the elevator up to the suite. Lenny was talking to the cameraman, but he turned when he heard Brendan approaching.

"Kaitlin will be right with us. Brendan," he said, smiling ruefully, "you need to powder your nose."

"So I hear," Brendan said wryly. He excused himself and went into the suite. The woman doing makeup was set up in one of the bedrooms, and he hesitated, knowing that Kaitlin was there, too.

Then the door opened and she came out. For a minute they were alone. Really alone.

Then her eyes narrowed, and her smile wasn't the least bit sweet. "Thanks a lot, O'Herlihy. You made me feel really cheap out there."

He swallowed the feelings that had been growing throughout the long day. "Sorry, O'Herlihy. But then again, if the shoe fits..."

"The shoe is just about to fly in your face, Brendan. I shouldn't pay you a thing! I should opt out of these weddings myself. And don't you dare call me O'Herlihy like that again. Don't—''

He stepped forward, clamping his hand over her mouth before she could go on. Her eyes rose to meet his in a cool blue fire of unreasonable fury.

"Kaitlin, may I remind you that you chose to keep the name. For your business, you said. And then you wanted an annulment from me—after all those years of keeping my name! So if I want to call you by it, I damn well will! And let me remind you of something else, too. You were willing to pay a hell of a lot to have your way the last time I saw you.''

She tried to bite him, but he moved his hand quickly, then pulled her against him. ''Damn you, Kaitlin!''

"Brendan, stop it! Let go of me! There are people right outside. We have to finish this shoot.''

"Oh, great! You're about to bite me, but when I fight back, you scream about propriety. You don't fight fair, lady, so don't expect fairness from me.''

"I didn't know that we were fighting,'' she snapped.

"I walked in, and you attacked.''

"You haven't been attacking all evening?''

All evening. She had been in his arms all evening. And she was in his arms now. He was growing tenser and hotter by the minute. It was worse than ever here. Worse, being alone.

He shook his head slowly, then he released her. "Let's go. Let's finish your damn commercial.''

She went very still, then she swept by him. When he started to follow her, she swung around and hissed, "Go powder your nose!"

He stopped, staring at her, as she continued. "If I'm paying you so damn well, I want my money's worth."

He arched a brow, smiling. "Oh, honey, you already *have* gotten your money's worth," he assured her.

But he swung around and stepped into the bedroom to have his makeup retouched, slamming the door behind him. When he came out, he allowed the door to slam behind him again. Then he was sorry he had. The girl, Janis, was obviously waiting for him. She jumped sky high at the crack of the door.

"Mr. O'Herlihy, they're ready for you. If you're ready, that is."

"Brendan. And I'm ready. Thanks."

She smiled nervously, still staring at him as he opened the outer door of the suite for her. She flushed. "How could she have divorced you?" she whispered.

"I wondered about that myself," he said, and smiled. "Come on, this is almost over."

Almost, but not quite. Lenny explained the scene to him. It was late, the end of a perfect day of sun and fun. And the evening was going to be even better, because they'd been doused in sunblock all day. No painful burns. No skin that couldn't bear to be touched.

"You're carrying her off for a night of ecstasy now. That's all you have to remember. Got it?"

"Oh, yeah, I've got it," Brendan said dryly.

Kaitlin was standing there. He took a step forward and lifted her off her feet. She gasped when he held her like a sack of potatoes. "Okay, Lenny, where am I supposed to be when I start looking forward to all this ecstasy?"

"Right there. Just stare into her eyes and come toward me."

Brendan walked to the end of the hall with Kaitlin in his arms. "Ecstasy, Kaitlin," he said sarcastically. "Remember, we're anticipating ecstasy."

"Yes, because the night really *is* almost over," she said.

"No talking, you two," Lenny called. "Just eyes, nothing but eyes. Okay, action. Roll 'em!"

Brendan started down the hallway. Eyes. Oh, yeah. Hers were the most delicate blue he had ever seen in his life. Eyes...but he could feel her fingertips at his nape. The beautiful sweeping skirt left her knees bare, and her elegant stockings were rubbing against his hip. He could feel the soaring heat of her body and the beating of his heart.

"Cut! Gosh, guys, I'm sorry, but we'll have to do it one more time. I just realized that there's a cord in the shot. Hey, get that out of there, huh?" he shouted to the nearest technician.

Kaitlin closed her eyes. "Damn! I thought we were done!"

"Hey, I'm the one doing all the work," Brendan reminded her curtly. "And you're not exactly a featherweight."

She kicked him, but he only held her closer. "Watch it, Ms. O'Herlihy. I'll drop you flat next time."

She narrowed her eyes. "You wouldn't dare."

"I dare anything, and you know it," he reminded her. She must have believed him, because her arms tightened around his neck. He smiled.

"Ready?" Lenny asked.

Brendan looked into her eyes again. "Yes."

Action . . . and the cameras rolled. Brendan walked with her to the door, then thrust it open with his foot before walking inside with her and closing the door behind him.

"Perfect!" Lenny called. "Perfect!"

They were alone in the room. She was still in his arms. And her eyes were still on his.

Slowly, very, very slowly, he eased her to her feet. Her body rubbed along the length of his, and it was torture.

Then she was standing on her own, and he knew he had to go.

"Dinner next Wednesday. I'll pick you up at eight. Be ready."

She nodded.

"I'll send the tux to your office," he said harshly.

She nodded again.

Almost blindly, he swung around. Then he felt her hand on his shoulder, and he turned back. "What?"

"If I'm so good at getting what I want," she said softly, wistfully, "why is it that nothing ever went right for us?"

He had no answer for her. He wasn't even sure she had really voiced the soft, painful question.

"You're not going to stand me up?"

"No."

He turned and opened the door, then hurried down the hall, heedless of Lenny calling to him. Heedless of everything.

The day was over. And he needed to get away.

On Friday morning Kaitlin came into the office and found Danny, Sam and Janis watching a preliminary version of the commercial in the conference room.

She stood in the back, watching the day unfold before her eyes, and wanted to scream. It was too painful to watch.

She wanted Brendan to be real so she could run to the screen and smack him right in the face. Ever since he had walked—no, swaggered, or at the very least sauntered—back into her life, thoughts of him had been plaguing her.

She had spent a night with Gram, looking for dresses, and Gram had found a beautiful creation in dove-gray silk and lace. But Kaitlin hadn't quite managed to be as enthusiastic as she felt she should have been.

Her mind had wandered.

And wandered.

And then there had been her dreams. Decadent dreams. Dreams so real she had woken up in a cold sweat.

She had always done things wholeheartedly. When she had been with Brendan, life had been a feast. And since they had parted...

She hadn't had a single real involvement, throwing herself into her work instead. She had dated, but she had never let anyone come close. Now she wished she had. She wished she'd had all kinds of experiences. Then she could have dealt much better with her feelings for Brendan.

Instead, all she did was dream of him.

Sometimes the dreams were wonderful. She could almost hear the laughter, the sighs.

Other times the dreams were painful. She would be walking in a mist, and then she'd find herself in the cemetery. Brendan would be standing there, and she'd call to him, but he wouldn't look up. And then, when he did look up, he'd look right through her, and no matter how loudly she called, he didn't seem to hear.

And sometimes she would relive the agony when she had lost the baby. Once again she was there all alone, hearing the doctor tell her there was no heartbeat. She wondered again how anything could hurt so much, and she called to him again. Again and again.

But he didn't come....

The lights went on, calling her back to reality. The sixty seconds were over. The voice-over had faded away. And everyone in the room was staring at her.

Danny was grinning from ear to ear. "Wow, boss! I have never seen anything so hot in all my born days!"

"My fingers are still sizzling!" Sam laughed.

"All right, all right!" Kaitlin groaned. "No more."

"I have sweat breaking out all over my body!" Danny said.

"Good! Because you're about to sweat your way to the unemployment office," she assured him.

She turned and left the room quickly, hurrying to her office and slamming the door. It was a great commercial. So why wasn't she in seventh heaven?

"Damn you, Brendan O'Herlihy!" she swore. Then she noticed that her private line was buzzing. She picked it up. "Yes, Sam?"

"Private call," Sam said quickly and hung up.

"Hello?" Kaitlin said. It was probably Gram or Barbara.

"Hello. Just checking on Wednesday."

It was Brendan. She held her breath, counted slowly, then spoke. "I never welsh on a payment."

"I'll remember that. See you then."

And he was gone.

It was the name O'Herlihy. Why had she kept it?

Brendan had been gone so long. They'd sent him to the Middle East. Even when she had realized that he wasn't coming back to be with her, she hadn't been able to file the divorce papers at first. She had spent long nights awake and miserable, realizing slowly that no matter how tender he had once been, he hadn't really wanted the cold, quick ceremony that had made them man and wife. It had just been for the baby. And now the baby was gone.

When he'd finally come home, he had been both distant and hungry, hungry as she'd never known him. The service had changed him; the things that he had seen had changed him. He had seemed to need her, but he hadn't talked, and he hadn't been able to listen, either. And then he'd gone again.

All she'd had left were school and her part-time job with an ad agency. And by the time she was twenty-one, she'd already acquired a very nice professional reputation as Kaitlin O'Herlihy.

She had kept the name for business purposes.

Or had she kept the name because she had really prayed all along that he wouldn't allow her to give it up, to give him up?

Kaitlin sighed, hesitated a moment, then sprang to her feet. She'd created a great ad, and she'd endured hell to do it. She deserved a break.

She left the office, stopping just long enough to tell Janis that she was in charge.

She spent the afternoon in a desperate flurry of shopping, then remembered just in time that Gram was bringing Mr. Rosen to dinner, and Barbara and Joe would be joining them, too.

And she didn't have a thing in the house for dinner, including the steaks she had told Gram she would make.

She bought the steaks, Idaho potatoes and the ingredients for a Caesar salad, then hurried home. She straightened the house quickly, then started the salad and the potatoes, watching the clock all the while.

When the doorbell rang, she swallowed a mouthful of wine and hurried to answer it.

It was Barbara and Joe. Kaitlin stepped aside quickly, welcoming her cousin with a warm embrace and giving Joe a big hug, too. They both seemed to have a glow about them. Barbara was beautiful to begin with, with her coppery curls and green eyes. And Joe was tall and lean, sandy-haired and hazel-eyed and very handsome. But tonight they both looked dazzling.

"You guys look great," she told them laughingly.

Barbara wiggled her hand beneath Kaitlin's nose. "It isn't us—it's the diamond. Oh, Kaitlin, isn't it beautiful?"

It was a beautiful diamond. Pear shaped, throwing off a million different colors in the light.

"Gorgeous," she agreed. "But the glow is coming from the two of you. Joe, I bought some champagne, want to crack it open? Gram is never late, she should be along any second."

"I'd love to crack open the champagne," Joe assured her. He and Barbara followed Kaitlin into the kitchen. "Kaitlin," he murmured, hesitating, then plunging in, "did Brendan come to see you?"

She managed to keep her smile. "Yes, he did."

Joe exhaled with relief. "Then everything is all right with you?"

"Of course," she said. "Here's the champagne." She heard the bell ring again. "And there's Gram. I'll bet she's glowing, too. I'm going to feel like a fifth wheel tonight. I'll be the only one not glowing." She grinned and started for the door, then paused, realizing that Joe and Barbara were staring at one another with nervous expressions.

"What?" she demanded.

Barbara shook her head. The bell was ringing more insistently.

"Barbara...?"

"I'll get the door," Barbara said.

"No, it's my house. I'll go," Kaitlin told her.

It was Gram. And she was with a tall, handsome older man with a full cap of white hair, dancing blue eyes to match Gram's, and a delightful smile. Kaitlin welcomed him warmly and urged them both in.

"Kaitlin, this is Al Rosen. Al, me granddaughter, Kaitlin O'Herlihy."

"Al!" Kaitlin took his hand, and she liked him immediately. He had a firm grip and that great smile. And he had given Gram a glow.

"Barbara and Joe are already here, in the kitchen. Joe is just opening the champagne."

"Just Barbara and Joe?" Gram asked. They were already through the entryway, with its high ceiling, by the kitchen door. Kaitlin stopped and looked at Gram inquisitively.

"Who else is coming?"

Joe was behind her, clearing his throat. "I was trying to tell you, Kaitlin. Your grandmother ran into Brendan this afternoon at our house."

She turned and stared at him. He grimaced and whispered, "Well, at least you're not going to be a fifth wheel." She didn't smile. "Kaitlin, I didn't invite him."

The doorbell was ringing again, and Al Rosen was looking at her with a question in his eyes. Should he get the door for her?

No . . . Gram wouldn't have done this to her!

Kaitlin hurried to the door and threw it open.

Gram had.

Brendan was standing there, wearing a red polo shirt and form-hugging jeans. And those glasses with the dark lenses that hid all his thoughts.

"No!" she whispered.

And then Barbara was beside her, laughing nervously. "Guess who's coming to dinner? Brendan, hi, come on in."

"Brendan!" It was Gram, coming forward. "Thank you for comin'. I'm so glad you made it." She turned to Kaitlin. "He told me that he couldna come, and I twisted his arm, I did. I assured him that ye'd be pleased, Kaitlin."

"Pleased as punch," Kaitlin managed to say.

Gram smiled delightedly. "Come on, Al, let's see to that champagne!"

She and Al Rosen disappeared through the swinging door to the kitchen, with Barbara nearly running at their heels.

And once again Kaitlin was alone with Brendan. "I thought I was supposed to see you on Wednesday!" she said.

He pulled off his glasses and leaned against the door frame. "You are. I just came tonight because I couldn't seem to resist your grandmother."

"The evening has just gone straight to hell!" Kaitlin groaned.

He grinned and sauntered past her. "Oh, I don't think so. I never did have a problem with your cooking. Steak, Joe tells me. Sounds like a good meal."

He started for the kitchen. At the swinging door he paused. "Coming, Ms. O'Herlihy?"

She closed the front door and leaned against it. He waited, and she groaned aloud. "Yes, I'm coming."

"I knew you'd see it my way."

She swept by him as regally as she could, pausing just before entering the kitchen. "Your way, Mr. O'Herlihy? This is *my* house and it's *my* party!" she informed him heatedly, then pushed through the door.

She managed to look at Joe casually and ask, "Is the champagne open?"

"It is. Ready for a glass?"

She glanced at Brendan. "I'm ready for a bottle," she said pleasantly, then accepted the glass that Joe had poured for her, draining it quickly.

She was in for another long night.

Chapter 4

There was a certain amount of chaos in the kitchen as the champagne was passed around, and Brendan met Al, and Joe greeted Brendan, and Barbara kissed Brendan like a long-lost relative. Then the noise level began to die down, and Barbara told Kaitlin that the table looked beautiful and that she would set another place for Brendan. Kaitlin drank her second glass of champagne, then a third, then she managed to shoo her grandmother and Al Rosen out of the kitchen so she could check on the meal. Joe, nearly as comfortable in her house as he was in his own, offered to show everyone the living room.

Kaitlin turned, only to find that she was rid of everyone except for her unexpected guest. He was standing at the refrigerator, pulling out the salad. She wanted to tell him to get out, but she poured herself another glass of champagne instead, watching him.

"Isn't that stuff still deadly for you?" he asked politely.

"I'm older," she said with a shrug. He let it go at that. He set the salad on the counter, along with the fixings for the dressing and the anchovies to be added at the last minute.

She brushed past him, wishing there was a little more room in her kitchen. "Wouldn't you like to go out and sit with the other guests? The invited ones?"

He leaned against the counter, grinning. "I thought I'd try to be helpful."

"If you'd really wanted to be helpful," she reminded him heatedly, "you would have turned down the invitation."

"How could I turn down your grandmother?"

"Oh, it might have taken some strength, but I'm sure you could have managed it."

He stepped past her, making himself at home and reaching into the refrigerator again. He rummaged around for a beer, popping it open as she stared at him. "I can only take so much champagne, no matter how great the celebration." He smiled.

She turned to her steaks, which were still marinating. She took them out of the mixture, set them on the broiler pan and put them into the oven. When she turned again, Brendan was finishing the salad. She let him, sweeping out of the room with the rolls and butter. Brendan followed her with the salad, and she went to turn the steaks. By the time she had pulled them out, everything else was already on the table. He took the platter from her to carry it out.

"You wanted me to turn down steaks?" he asked softly. "I'll give you this—you always did broil a great steak."

"And I'll give you this," she replied sweetly. "You..." She hesitated, knowing that what she was about to say was true. "You were always good at helping out in the kitchen."

"Was that a compliment?" he asked her.

She shrugged, then smiled. "No, that was probably four glasses of champagne." She walked out, and he followed with the platter. She called to everyone else, and they came to the table.

Ten minutes later, Kaitlin was glad of the champagne. She was feeling mellow, something she hadn't thought possible. Not with Brendan at her table.

But she realized that he and Joe and Barbara were very comfortable together. As comfortable as she was with them herself. And she knew then that they had seen a lot of Brendan—and that they had just been careful not to mention it to her.

As for Gram, she had always doted on Brendan. And Al Rosen had seemed to like him right away, too. Brendan had a way with people. Gaelic charm with a soft New England accent, she decided. Al Rosen, it seemed, was a passionate boat enthusiast. And few people knew the Eastern seaboard better than Brendan.

Brendan told Al about his latest project, searching for a small Spanish man-of-war that had been blown off course and probably sunk near the Upper Keys in the late fifteen hundreds. When Al told him wistfully that it sounded like the dream of a lifetime and a great way to make a living, Brendan cast Kaitlin a quick glance.

"Some might see it as modern-day piracy," he murmured politely.

She smiled back. "Some might."

She really had bought good champagne. And the ice bucket was right next to her. It was easy to reach for more. And it was nice. She didn't feel in the least as if she had over imbibed. She felt comfortably drowsy. Content. Able to weather any storm.

Including her ex-husband.

"So tell us more about the wedding," Brendan said to Gram, deftly drawing the others into the conversation.

Gram flushed. "Well, Kaitlin and I bought my dress the other night."

"It's beautiful. Really beautiful," Kaitlin said, smiling at Al.

"And simple. Like our ceremony will be. Some of the family will be coming, and a few close friends," Gram said. She and Al smiled at one another, and Kaitlin felt her heart warming.

"Well," Joe teased, "it sounds like a wild fling to me!"

"A marriage is always a wild fling," Al said, his eyes on Gram. "But as for the wedding..."

"I had my big wedding," Gram said softly. "When I married Granda. We had nothing in Dublin, really nothing at'all. But me mum made me gown, and me sisters sewed the pearls onto the train. And Da's best friend was a butcher, so he gave us a grand reception out in the yard. It was a great wedding, though, a wonderful wedding. Like the kind Barb and Joe will have. And that's good, Al, eh? But not for us. It's the marriage that matters."

"Your wedding will be beautiful, Gram," Barbara assured her.

Brendan reached across the table for the red wine and poured a small portion into his glass. "But I agree with Liz," he said softly. "It's not the wedding but the marriage that counts."

He was looking at Kaitlin, and she wanted to slap him. She had wanted a big wedding, sure. But she had loved him. Really loved him with her whole heart. When they had been married in the midst of all the chaos, she had wanted it to last forever.

He was the one who hadn't wanted her when it came down to it.

She turned away from him coldly. "Well, here's to Gram and Al! May you live long and happily. Al, we're pleased to have you with us!"

"Here, here!" Joe said.

They all raised their glasses, and Gram and Al were duly toasted. Then Joe told them how hard it had been to get the church date he had wanted, and Barbara watched him with a soft smile. Kaitlin was still amazed that Joe had made the arrangements with the church.

"We need to go out looking for dresses," Kaitlin reminded her.

"Yes! How about this week?"

"Sure."

"How's your Wednesday night?"

"It's fine—" she began, then she felt Brendan watching her. How could she have forgotten? "Wednesday is bad for me," she said sweetly. "Tuesday?"

"How about Thursday?"

"Fine. I need something to wear for Gram and Al's wedding, so we can look for that at the same time."

"Sounds great," Barbara said. "I'm going to have to look pretty hard. I need something that's already in."

"Why can't you just order what you want?" Joe asked her.

She glanced at Kaitlin, shaking her head impatiently. "It can take a full year for a dress to be ordered and come in. There's usually a minimum of three to four months. I don't want to worry. I know there's something really beautiful out there, and I can just have it altered. Right, Kaitlin?"

Kaitlin nodded. Barbara poured more wine. "Of course, you do have to be careful. They've been having the strangest problem in Massachusetts. Donna was telling me about it the other day. There's a group of wedding bandits stealing shipments of gowns. Can you imagine?''

"Stealing wedding gowns?'' Brendan said. "What for?''

"They change the labels and sell them in the South and out in the West. Lots of women want to buy gowns more quickly than they can be specially made. It's quite a racket, I understand.''

"Well, if we're buying a gown to be altered,'' Kaitlin said, "at least we shouldn't have to worry. We'll find the gown if it takes all week, buy it and get a seamstress working on it right away.''

Barbara had finished her meal, so she pushed back her chair and picked up her plate. She dusted a kiss on Gram's hair. "Not all week,'' she said with a soft smile. "Don't forget, we have plans for Saturday.''

"Saturday. So close,'' Gram breathed.

"You can't be nervous!'' Kaitlin told her.

"Not too nervous, I hope!'' Al Rosen said.

They all laughed, and Kaitlin stood with Barbara to start picking up the dishes. She was dismayed to realize that she was swaying a little. She steadied herself on the chair and was certain that no one had caught her unintended movement.

Except for Brendan. He was watching her. Disapprovingly, she was certain.

Well, what and when she chose to drink was none of his affair.

"I'll help clear,'' Gram said.

"You'll do no such thing," Kaitlin told her. "You sit with Al, and we'll have cake and coffee coming right out."

She turned and carefully carried her collection of plates into the kitchen. She turned, expecting to find Barb behind her.

Brendan was there instead. He set a stack of dishes on the counter. "Want me to take the cake out?"

"I can take it out."

"I'd love to do it for you."

"You think that I've been—"

"Drinking too much champagne, yes. But hey, it's your house, your party. I just thought you might want someone else to carry the cake."

She plugged in the coffeepot. "Carry the cake, then. Make yourself happy."

He went out with it. Then Barb appeared with the last of the dishes, her eyes sparkling. "Well?"

"Well what? Oh, Mr. Rosen! I think he's charming. And he loves Gram, which is all that really matters, isn't it?"

"I'm not talking about Al! He *is* great. We liked him from the moment we met him—Joe and I. But what else would you expect from Gram other than a super guy?"

"Right," Kaitlin agreed, pulling out her best cups and saucers and cake plates. Then she paused and looked at Barb. "So what were you talking about?"

"You and Brendan."

Kaitlin stared at the coffee cups. "Brendan and me? We're adults. We'll manage."

"You'll manage?" Barbara said. "That's all?"

Kaitlin swung around and looked at her cousin. "Of course. You want me to be a bridesmaid, and I will. Even if Brendan's going to be there, too. Joe and Brendan have apparently seen a lot more of one another over the years than I realized. Maybe I should have known, though. After all, Joe did find him for me when I wanted to talk to him several years ago."

There must have been a trace of bitterness in her voice, because Barbara sighed. "And he wouldn't agree to have the marriage annulled. I'm sorry, Kaitlin, we both thought that if you just talked to him . . . well, Joe managed to get one very easily. And I did want to be married in the church. Not that it really matters. Married is married, just like Al said. The wedding goes by so quickly! But then you have the memories all your life. Kaitlin, I've waited so long! I do want a big wedding. I want a million people, and I want to be beautiful!"

Kaitlin smiled, then hugged her. "Joe wants you to have it all. It took him a while to come around, I'll grant you. But he seems to want it all to be perfect now."

Barbara nodded happily. "Just like you originally planned, before you and Brendan had that awful fight over that guy you were seeing." She paused, then gasped in horror. "Oh! I'm sorry, Kaitlin, I—"

"I wasn't seeing another guy," Kaitlin said wearily. "I told you that—"

"I know, I know, I'm so sorry! But that's what Brendan thought, wasn't it?"

"I guess. Barbara, it doesn't matter. It's all in the past."

"Oh, Kaitlin! I'm just so grateful to you both! It's so important for me to have you, and so important to Joe to have Brendan, too. And you've both been wonderful, trying to make it all just right for us."

"No problem," Kaitlin said, then turned away. The coffee was ready.

"I'll take out the cups," Barbara said. As she headed for the door she called back, "Joe put the liqueurs and the whiskey out. Did you get whipped cream? It's a great night for Irish coffee!"

"It sure is," Kaitlin agreed. She opened the refrigerator and found whipped cream. When she closed the door and turned again, Brendan was in the kitchen. Watching her.

"Want some help?" he asked. His gaze was fathomless, wandering up and down the length of her, then meeting her eyes.

She smiled. Sweetly. Defiantly. "Yes, please. Grab the cream and sugar and the coffeepot."

He did, still watching her as she sailed past him with the whipped cream.

The cake was wonderful, and Irish coffee went with it just right. Kaitlin had two cups.

Gram talked about her reception, and Barbara and Joe sat with their fingers entwined atop the table, listening, silently planning their own wedding. Kaitlin was surprised—then guilt-stricken—to find that her parents were coming down for the wedding. They would be arriving at the airport Friday afternoon.

"I said you'd pick them up, Kaitlin. Your mother will verify times with you sometime this week," Gram said.

"Of course," Kaitlin murmured.

Brendan, and now her parents. What more could she ask for? Oh, she loved her parents dearly, but she wasn't sure she wanted to be with them and Brendan in the same room, and she was certain that Gram had already invited Brendan to the wedding.

It didn't really matter, she decided. The champagne was curling around the whiskey in the Irish coffee. Or maybe the whiskey was curling around the champagne. It was going to be all right. Even if Brendan was at her dining room table, still staring at her. She smiled at him. He really did have those wonderful Irish good looks, with his ebony hair and beautiful green eyes, just sparked by those touches of gold. She wondered if life might not have been incredibly easier if she hadn't fallen so hard for him so long ago. It still seemed impossible that he was sitting in her dining room. And that she could smile so easily as he sat there!

Kaitlin realized then that Barbara had picked up most of the dishes, and Joe was standing behind her, saying that they had to leave.

Gram and Mr. Rosen were standing, too, and Brendan with them. She stood, and she wasn't sure if she swayed, or if she just thought that she did. At least she was still speaking rationally and coherently; she was certain of that.

But when she touched her lips, she had to press hard to make sure they were still there.

She ignored the feeling to smile and kiss Gram and Barbara and Joe goodbye, then she shook Al Rosen's hand. Then they were gone, and when she turned, she realized that Brendan was still in the house.

She didn't say anything. She just leaned against the door, watching him.

"Want me to leave?" he asked.

She smiled. "I'm not sure."

"Um," he murmured. His lashes seemed inky black, shielding his eyes. "Why don't you sit down in the living room? I'll pick up the rest of the dishes."

"There's a dishwasher."

"I know. I saw it. Do you want me to brew another pot of coffee?"

"I think I've had enough coffee."

"I think you've had enough *Irish* coffee. You might just need some of the strong black stuff."

His hand was on her arm, and he was leading her to the living room couch. She sat, and he slipped off her shoes. She felt his fingers against the arch of her foot, and she stared into his eyes.

She smiled. "Do you know, Brendan, you're still extraordinarily good-looking."

"Am I? Thank you." He shoved her back until she was leaning against the overstuffed arm of the chesterfield. Her eyes were very wide, her smile sweet, and her hair fell like Rapunzel's, in long, soft tresses and waves. His eyes caught hers. "And you're still extraordinarily beautiful, Kaitlin. But then, you know that, don't you?"

"I'm getting old, Brendan."

"All of thirty."

She shook her head. "It's young if you've done something with your life. I haven't really done anything with mine."

"You've done lots with your life. You've got a great business. You're bright, creative, talented. You've succeeded. That meant an awful lot to you between the ages of twenty and twenty-two."

She stared at him searchingly. "I didn't think you noticed anything I was feeling in those years," she said lightly.

He sighed. "Kaitlin... Never mind. I'm going to make coffee and finish your dishes."

"You don't have to. I can do them in the morning."

"Kaitlin, you're going to have a horrible headache in the morning. You're going to wish that someone would come along and shoot you."

She closed her eyes, vaguely aware that he was right. "It's all your fault."

"What's my fault?"

"The champagne. I inhaled it because you walked in."

She didn't see his crooked smile as he walked away. She winced slightly, aware that he had been right. She couldn't drink champagne. She'd never been able to. And she'd already suffered one wretched hangover this week. Now she was going to have another.

The room was heaving. Her eyes were closed, but the room was heaving. Like an ocean, undulating around her. She could feel her foot where he had touched her. Just her foot.

When they'd filmed the commercial, he'd touched a lot more than her foot. And she had felt that, too....

But tonight, despite her intoxicated state, she was feeling more. She was seeing more. She'd never heard his voice quite so clearly, felt it dance along her spine so seductively.

She liked it. She felt caressed by it, beguiled by it. She thought about the other day on the beach. She had wanted to touch his chest, to feel the thick, dark hair that grew there in such a fascinating pattern.

She wanted to curl against him. She wanted to taste his kiss.

She wanted to do more than that.

Something moved over her cheek. He was sitting beside her, stroking her face lightly with his knuckles.

She smiled. She had dreamed him, and he had appeared.

"Hi," she murmured.

"Hi. The coffee is done."

"Great." She couldn't stop smiling as she caught his hand and inspected it. She liked the broad back with its slight spattering of freckles. She liked his fingers, too. They were rugged hands, but handsome. Masculine hands. And when they touched her . . .

"I think I should just put you to bed," he said huskily.

She smiled. "Are you coming with me?"

He swore softly. "Damn it, Kaitlin, don't do this to me."

"That's right," she said huskily. "You said you weren't going to seduce me."

"Right."

"That's so honorable of you, Brendan."

He sighed. "Kaitlin, you may not believe this, but I was always trying to do the honorable thing. I've never known how to explain the way I felt after Sean died. I know that I was at fault, and I have no excuse. I can only apologize."

Tears were coming to her eyes. She didn't want to get weepy. She was feeling so content and peaceful, so delicious and peaceful. . . .

And hungry.

She set his hand against her cheek and closed her eyes. "I loved Sean, too, you know," she said softly. "Not the way you did, of course. I understood. I really did.'' Her eyes flew open, and she smiled. ''Brendan, did I tell you that you've aged well?''

''Just like fine wine,'' he returned with a grin.

She sat up, curled her arms around his neck and met his gaze. She studied his eyes. And then it seemed too hard to resist, and she pulled him close to her. She had wanted to do it all day when they were filming.

She kissed him.

At first he stiffened, his mouth closed. But when she teased his lips with the tip of her tongue, prodding slightly, he gave in to her. He opened his mouth and seemed to consume her. Hot, sweet, searing, his tongue plunged deeply into her mouth, where it met and dueled with her own. When he broke the kiss it was only to press his lips against her ear, laving it, then the pulse at the base of her throat, tasting and feeling and savoring. Then his mouth fused with hers once again.

This was the kiss they had known before, only deeper, hungrier. More demanding and more giving. Her body trembled and shook. She moved her fingers into his hair, to touch and explore. Then she allowed her nails to trail down his back, her fingers tugging at his shirt, freeing it from his waistband so she could touch his hot flesh. She moved her hands from his back around to his chest and allowed her fingers to tease the crisp black mat that had so fascinated her the other day.

His mouth lifted from hers. ''Kaitlin, I'm warning you . . .''

She found his lips again and pulled him down. The little pearl buttons on her white silk blouse were giving, melting away. His hands were on her, hefting the weight of her breasts, teasing them through her bra. And then he was freeing her flesh from its restraint. His palms moved over her nipples, and then his dark head lowered against her, and he was tasting her, filling his mouth with the hardness of one nipple, with the soft flesh and supple firmness of her breast. And she was clinging to him, soft gasps escaping her as she held him close.

His head rose, hair tousled, his look sensual. He lifted her, cast aside the blouse and the bra and laid her back, his eyes studying and devouring her. She wanted him so badly. And she loved the way he looked at her. Just like he had before...

"What you're doing to me should be illegal," he whispered to her raggedly. "Punishable by death."

She smiled and tried to reach for him. Her fingers caressed his tousled hair; then her arms fell to her sides.

He rose and lifted her into his arms. He moved down the hallway to her bedroom, where he carried her into the darkness and laid her down, tearing at the covers as he did so.

"Brendan!" she whispered.

His hands were on the zipper of her skirt. She could feel his touch against her bare flesh, and it was delicious. In the shadows she could see his eyes, could see the passion and determination within them, and she smiled again. He was with her, holding her.

"We should have made it," she told him vaguely. "We came from the same background, the same religion, the same ideals, the same desires. And I loved you so much. What happened to us, Brendan?"

Her breath was soft against his cheek. Her body was supple and liquid and beautiful, offering all the torments of hell and all the raptures of heaven.

A harsh, ragged moan escaped him as his lips fell lightly on her forehead, then her lips. And she felt the soft hair on his chest and the warm ripple of muscle beneath her fingers.

Kaitlin felt his lips on her own, his hands on her nakedness.

He rose and looked at her, then swore at the tension that gripped his body.

She was so damn beautiful, curled on the bed.

He swallowed hard, then tucked in his shirttails and did up his buttons. Her lashes were thick and lustrous against her cheeks, her hair a wild tangle. There was a stray lock over her cheek, and he reached tenderly to move it. His hand hovered, then he stroked her cheek gently again.

"Yes, we should have made it, Kaitlin. We should have made it."

Then he bent and kissed her lips once again. A soft sigh escaped her, and she smiled as she slipped into sleep.

Then he smiled as he pulled the sheet over her. She was going to have one hell of a morning.

He knew her well. And she was definitely going to have one hell of a morning.

Chapter 5

Kaitlin's head was spinning, and her tongue felt like sandpaper.

For the first few minutes as she began to wake up, all she could do was feel the subtle tortures within her body.

And from there on it only got worse.

There was a sheet covering her to her neck, but she felt funny beneath it.

She was naked.

And she wasn't one of those people who naturally slip naked into bed.

A groan escaped her, and she tried to remember the evening.

Brendan.

It could all be explained with a single word. He had arrived, and she had drained a glass of champagne in a fraction of a second. And more had followed. Then there had been dinner and cake and coffee. Irish coffee.

She groaned aloud again. She should have been born a devout Muslim. Muslims didn't drink at all, did they? She would never have tasted champagne in the first place.

Never, never again.

She tried to sit up, her head pounding. She wanted someone to shoot her and put her out of her misery.

To shoot her...

Someone had said something about that last night. That she would wake up with a headache so bad that she would want to be shot.

Brendan...

Oh, no. There had been dinner, then conversation and Irish coffee. That was where she had stopped before. Because she didn't really want to go on.

She had stood at the door. She had kissed Gram and Barbara good night. She had hugged Joe. She had waved to her almost step-grandfather. Then she had closed the door, and...

Brendan.

He had still been inside. He had brought her to the couch. He had said something about the dishes and coffee, and she had closed her eyes, and he had come back.

A very, very loud groan broke from her lips.

She hadn't been able to keep herself from telling him how good he looked. How well he had weathered time. He'd promised not to seduce her, but he'd also warned her that he couldn't be responsible if she seduced him.

And, oh! The things she could remember! Curling her fingers into his hair, welcoming—inviting—his kiss. And feeling his touch on her.

She could even remember that he had carried her in here, already half naked, and removed her skirt.

What else had happened?

Her memory was blanking out on her. It was as if she had forgotten everything after reaching the darkness of the room.

Rather evident, isn't it, Kaitlin? she tormented herself in silence, her head crashing painfully to the pillow. Then she rose, wishing she could just stay in bed forever. If only her head would stop pounding so badly! No, no, maybe it was good that her head was pounding, because she really didn't want to think.

She had to take something for her head.

She realized that she was naked and wrapped the sheet around herself.

Her clothing was tossed over the big wicker chair in the corner of the room. Her shoes were beneath it.

She staggered into the kitchen and discovered that everything was as neat as a pin. The coffeepot was cleaned out, with coffee measured into it so all she had to do this morning was flick a switch. She didn't. Not yet. She didn't want to wake up.

She fumbled through the cabinets for a packet of bicarbonate, mixed it with water and swallowed the concoction in seconds. She set the glass on the counter, her thoughts suddenly all too clear.

What a fool I am, she thought derisively. I meet him every four years and hop into bed, then spend the rest of my life dreaming. How could I have done such a thing! I'm thirty years old. Mature. I should be able to handle this, to pretend it never happened.

But she couldn't. Because there would be dinner Wednesday. And Gram's wedding. And parties. And more weddings.

She could beg out of dinner. She could be deathly ill all week. She felt as if she was deathly ill already.

With another moan, she staggered to the bedroom and crawled into bed, praying for sleep to claim her again. It did, but it was anything but restful, because she began to dream.

It was years ago, almost four years ago. She was home, and one of her cousins mentioned that another cousin had gotten an annulment so she could be married again in the church. Kaitlin's mother had been there, and she had mentioned softly that if only Kaitlin and Brendan had gotten an annulment, they both could have looked forward to marrying again within the church.

Her father had suggested that her mother lead her own life, but Kaitlin had seen the hurt and the hope in her mother's eyes.

Then Joe, good old Joe, had known where to find Brendan. He had set up a meeting, and she had driven down to the Keys to see Brendan.

He'd been surprised to see her. Cold, aloof. Then he'd made an about face, asking her to stay for dinner. He'd cooked for her at his house on the water, and she'd had to admit that the surroundings were really elegant. And there had been candlelight, and wine....

She could remember everything in her dream. The room had been beautifully paneled in light wood. There had been a rose on the table, a snowy cloth and beautiful crystal. And Brendan. When she saw him, she started drinking the wine too quickly. The food was delicious, but she barely touched it. He was charming, his green eyes ablaze in the candlelight. He asked about her family, and she asked about his. They talked about his latest venture, and she told him she was thinking about breaking away from her firm to form her own company. She flirted—outrageously, probably. But it was so easy to do, so natural. And then she began to explain why she had come, and why an annulment would benefit both of them. He listened, and she didn't notice his eyes narrowing. Then he suggested a stroll along the deck, over the water.

In the dream the mist was all around him, but she could still feel the balmy salt air, smell the rich scent of the sea—and the man. She didn't know when she stopped talking, except that it must have been when he kissed her. When he moved his lips over her bare shoulders. And she knew that she wasn't talking when he lifted her into his arms. And she knew what was happening, but she had no desire to stop it. He was seducing her, and the torment was sweet. Suddenly they were inside, and there was moonlight streaming into the room. She held her breath against the feel of his lips moving slowly over the glow-bathed length of her, until the longing became so strong that she was unable to endure it. The desperate desire for fulfillment, for the raw tempest and passion, rose within her, and she touched him, whispering incoherent words against his flesh. It was so good to feel him inside her again that tears came to her eyes.

He touched her again during the night. And again.

But in the morning she woke up alone. He had left a note saying that she should come back when all she wanted was him. And she had known then that he had played her so damn well that she didn't dare go back, ever.

The mist faded. She could hear a clock ticking. She was awake, but the dream had been so real that patches of it remained.

No, the dream only seemed to have been so real because of everything that had happened last night.

At least her head wasn't pounding so badly. She cracked one eye open.

She was going to live.

Then she realized that she could smell coffee. And she sensed that she was not alone. She sensed it so strongly that she screamed when she rolled over and discovered that there was a figure in the doorway.

"For God's sake, Kaitlin, it's me."

"Brendan!"

The sheet had fallen. It was down to her waist, and she was gaping at him.

She grabbed madly for the sheet.

What for? He had apparently gotten her into her present state of undress. Or else she had done it herself because of him.

She swore and leaped out of bed, trying to cloak herself in the sheet. "Damn it, Brendan, of all the nerve! I should call the police. After everything you did—"

One ebony brow shot up. "Everything I did?" he interrupted politely.

"Oh!" She spun around and stamped into her bathroom, locking the door behind her. She should have gotten rid of him. She should have told him to leave the house.

All she wanted now was a shower. To soak herself. To drown.

No, no, she had to get a grip on herself. He was in her house. Maybe he'd never left. No, she'd been awake, and he'd been gone. Besides, he was dressed in tennis shorts and a sweatshirt, and he had that just bathed and shaved look about him. He'd been gone, but he'd come back. Why?

She let the water pour over her, easing her tension. Then she panicked again.

He had promised her that he wouldn't seduce her.

And he hadn't, she reminded herself. She had to be honest with herself. With him. She had to be cold and firm and dignified. She had to admit that it had been her fault, but that it could never, never happen again.

She turned off the water with a jerk and left the shower, then rigorously toweled her hair dry. She met her reflection in the large mirror over the sink. Her eyes were huge.

And bloodshot.

She reached into the cabinet for her makeup and did a quick repair job. Her fingers were trembling, and she was certain that she was going to have mascara down her nose, but it wasn't so bad.

She tied her terry robe around herself and stepped into the bedroom.

He wasn't there, and her door was closed. She bit her lower lip, then dressed quickly in jeans and a soft knit shirt. She brushed her hair, convinced herself that she didn't look nearly as green as she felt and turned toward the door.

She had to stand there for several seconds before she could bring herself to twist the knob. She was going to be strong, mature, aloof. She was going to—oh, hell.

She managed to leave the room at last. Brendan was at the dining room table, sipping coffee and reading the morning paper. He looked exceptionally awake and aware. Clean and fresh and masculine.

And surely he was gazing at her in a condescending fashion.

She walked to the table and curled her fingers around the wooden frame of one of the chairs.

"Why did you come back?" she asked him sharply.

"Why are you so angry?" he questioned in return, leaning back in his chair, arms crossed over his chest.

"I'm not angry."

His eyes widened in disbelief, and he lifted her keys from the table. "The only way I could bolt your door was from the outside. But I thought you might like these back."

"Oh," she said numbly. "Well, thank you." *I think,* she added in silence.

"The coffee is hot."

She nodded. Coffee. Maybe after one cup she could get rid of him. She walked into the kitchen, poured herself a cup, added sugar and milk generously and drank it right there in the kitchen. She poured herself another cup and went more lightly on both the cream and the sugar, then squared her shoulders and swung around to return to the dining room to face him again.

Except that she didn't have to return to the dining room. He was leaning on the doorway, watching her, smiling.

"You're gulping that stuff down just like you were inhaling the champagne last night," he commented.

"Thank you for noticing," she said.

He was still smiling. "You really shouldn't be mad at me."

Mad? She was pale white and wanted to crawl under a rock. She lifted her chin. Mature, dignified.

"I'm not angry with you, Brendan. Really. You did...you did promise me..."

"Yes?"

She wasn't white anymore. She was flaming red. If only she could speak! She was never going to manage mature and dignified if she couldn't talk.

"You did promise not to seduce me."

"Yes, I did."

"And I know..."

"Yes?" he asked.

"Well, I know that what happened was my fault. That I, uh..."

He leaned more comfortably against the door frame.

"You're not making this easy, you know."

"No, I wouldn't think of it. I'm enjoying it way too much."

"It can't happen again!" she cried desperately.

"What can't happen? I didn't do anything."

She set her coffee cup down and curled her fingers around the countertop behind her. "Brendan, I've admitted that. And I'm not angry, really I'm not."

"You shouldn't be. You should be grateful."

"Grateful!"

"I picked up the place. I locked you in all nice and sound."

"Yes, yes, you locked the door. Thank you. Great. It was before you locked the door that I'm talking about."

"Yes?"

Damn it. He was having a good time. At her expense.

"I was responsible. It was my fault. But it isn't going to happen again."

"Just exactly what is it that isn't going to happen again?"

"Brendan, please!"

He arched his brows. "Seriously. I'd like to know."

She swore softly, picked up her coffee and pushed past him to take a seat at the table. He followed and stood behind her, making her very uneasy.

"Let's see. My memory is probably better than yours."

"Brendan, stop."

"Not on your life. Let's see, I got you to the sofa, I got the dishes in the dishwasher, and I put the coffee on. And then I came out and sat next to you. And then..." His husky whisper teased her ear as he leaned behind her, putting his hands on the table. "And then, wow. Kaitlin, you have a kiss that singes the hair."

"Brendan..."

"And then, you know what?"

"I don't want to know what!"

"Then your hands were all over me. In my hair, on my shoulders, touching me...and I was trying so hard to be noble, but you've got a great smile. And great eyes. And really great—"

"Brendan!"

"And I just couldn't resist. So there we were on the couch, and the next thing I knew, half your clothing was off. And you were ripping at my shirt—"

"I was not!"

"You were, I swear it. And your fingers were all over my chest and across my shoulders, then down my back. It was the most incredible, exquisite torture!" He slid around beside her and set his hand over hers. She tried to pull away, but he took her fingers between his hands, his thumb rubbing over her palm. "Just thinking about it right now, this very second...there's a cold sweat breaking out on my skin, and a hot rush sweeping through me—"

"Stop it!"

But he ignored her, pressing on. "I got you into the bed. And I kept telling myself that I had promised—promised!—not to seduce you. But you're such a flirt. Hot and sexy—and sweet. So there you were in bed, half dressed. I couldn't leave you that way."

Her eyes were wide on his, her expression one of absolute horror. She wanted to pull her hand away, but she couldn't. She wanted to scream, to hide beneath the table, but she couldn't do that, either.

"I touched you, and oh, Kaitlin, you moved so nicely. Your skirt just slid free in my hand. And your stockings came off, and then I..."

His voice trailed away as he shuddered. She stared at him, open-mouthed and paralyzed.

Then he dropped her hand and grinned disarmingly. "Then I threw the sheet over you, locked up and left."

"What!" She gasped.

He stood, still grinning. "I really did have to try very hard to be noble. But that was it, Kaitlin. I undressed you, put you to bed and left. You haven't sold your soul—or anything else, for that matter. For the moment, at least."

She stared at him blankly for a second; then her temper soared, and she stood to face him, her fingers wound so tightly into her palms that her nails were clawing into her flesh.

"What?"

"Kaitlin, I said that you didn't—"

She approached him in a fury, her left fist flying. He caught her wrist, swearing at her strength as he struggled to capture her tightly against him.

"Kaitlin, I said—"

"You said! You let me sit there and talk and stumble and nearly die of humiliation and shame. And you knew all along—"

"Well, of course, I knew! I wasn't the inebriated one. And, as a matter of fact," he added, his green gaze dangerously alight, "I was rather insulted that you could even imagine that we had gone through with anything. I could never have forgotten a single one of our sexual encounters. No matter what I'd been drinking."

"Oh!" She gritted her teeth and tried to free her wrists. When she couldn't, she tried to kick him, but he stepped back quickly, maintaining his grip on her.

"Come on, Kaitlin."

"You just sat there and let me think—"

"Kaitlin, you were thinking about a lot that was true! You did try damn hard to seduce me. And it was hard to resist you, too. But I did."

"Congratulations!" she snapped.

He laughed, brought her wrists together and pushed her into her chair.

"Want to know why I did?" he asked her.

"I'm just dying to hear!"

"Good, because you're going to. I don't want you to have any champagne excuses."

"Champagne—"

"You see, Kaitlin, I did play hardball against you once. When I realized that you had come to see me just because you wanted me to participate in a lie—"

"Brendan, it would have been for both of us!"

He let out an expletive that told her precisely what he thought of that, then continued heatedly. "Listen, we played this badly once. I seduced you because you wanted something. Then you tried to seduce me because I was the only one in the house—"

"What a horrible thing to say!" she interrupted furiously.

Suddenly he didn't seem angry anymore. He laughed, his hold on her hands loosening, and his eyes

were bright. "Okay, does that mean you tried to seduce me because I was me?"

She groaned softly, trying to pull away from his
touch. "Brendan, please!"

"All right, it doesn't matter for the moment. What
I'm trying to explain is why I held back last night when
you were doing your best to be a nearly irresistible
temptation. When we make love, I want it to be for the
right reasons. I don't want you even slightly inebriated. And I don't want you thinking that you can
bargain anything from me."

"I never did!" she flared.

He shrugged. "All right. But you never came
back."

"You made a fool out of me—and then left."

"We both did some pretty sad things to one another over the years. But, Kaitlin, I still want you.
More than ever. But if I'm going to have you, I want
you to want me with your eyes wide open."

"Brendan, I told you that it can't—"

"Can't ever happen again. But it can, Kaitlin." He
stood, grinning. "And I'm willing to bet that it will."

Her eyes flashed sharply. "You're not allowed to
seduce me, remember."

"I remember. But I'm willing to bet that you de-
cide to seduce me again—stone cold sober."

"Not a chance," she said sweetly.

"We'll see," he told her. "It really was one hell of
a night. I could have told you more, but . . ."

"You told me quite enough!"

He laughed and headed toward the door. "See you Wednesday night, Kaitlin. At eight."

"Maybe."

"Be ready," he warned. He allowed the door to slam shut behind him.

The sound caused her ragged nerves to snap, and she jumped, then smacked a hand on the table. "Damn him!" she swore aloud. But swearing gave her a headache all over again. She leaned her face flat on the table and savored the coolness of the wood.

Well, at least they hadn't made love.

Did that really make it any better? After everything she had done?

She lifted her head. Damn him. She wasn't sure whether she was relieved or insulted that he had managed to refuse her invitation.

She hadn't been able to refuse him....

But he thought that she would issue him another invitation. Well, that would be a cold day in hell, she swore to herself silently. Never. Never! Too many things lay between them, things that could not be forgotten.

Then she trembled suddenly, remembering his words. He had said that he wanted her, that he wanted her more now than he ever had.

She wanted him, too. She always had.

And she was afraid that she always would.

"Ah, Kaitlin, me girl, we canna always have what we want!" she told herself aloud, mimicking Gram.

"What we want, love, isna always so good for us, eh?"

Brendan was definitely not good for her.

And still . . .

She groaned and rose. Brendan made good coffee, and there was almost a whole pot of it left in the kitchen. No sense in letting good coffee go to waste.

By Sunday she felt like living again. Barbara called and asked her to come over. She was about to say yes, then hesitated.

"Barbara, is Brendan going to be there?"

Barbara hesitated, and Kaitlin knew that he was. "He and Joe will be watching the football game. We can ignore them and look through the bridal magazines out by the pool."

She was about to say no, but then Barbara began to plead. "Kaitlin, please! Help me get things going!"

"All right. But I can't stay late."

Later on, she prided herself on that Sunday. Everything went very much as she planned.

Joe and Brendan did stay in the den, watching the football game. And she and Barbara stretched out by the pool and leafed through magazines, then looked through the menu for the hall that they had booked.

At six, the men and women joined one another at the kitchen counter for hot dogs and chili and beer.

At least, the others had beer. Kaitlin had a ginger ale. And she noticed that Brendan's inky lashes covered his eyes when he watched her now and then with amusement, and that his mouth curved with humor. But he didn't say anything. And neither did she.

They were polite to one another. Painfully polite. And she was very careful to keep a wide distance between them.

She had walked over, and she was determined to walk home. When she started off, she turned and looked back, certain that Brendan would be following her.

He wasn't.

She started walking again, then started violently when a hand fell on her shoulder. She swung around. Brendan smiled.

"Sorry, I—"

"Brendan, I've got an early morning tomorrow."

"So have I, Kaitlin. I just wanted to let you know that I booked Donna's favorite country club for the Saturday after your grandmother's wedding."

"What?"

"I managed to get a booking for a mixed shower. The Saturday following your grandmother's wedding. Is that all right? Can you manage it?"

"I—yes, I think so."

"Good. We can go over details at dinner."

"Fine."

"I'll let Donna know. It's what she and Bill wanted, a party with all their friends. Male and female."

She had always known that if and when Donna planned a wedding, she would want something with everyone together, rather than a shower with just the women. Kaitlin should have thought of it herself. She really couldn't complain that Brendan had done so.

He was staring at her, waiting. "Was there something else?" she asked defensively.

He shook his head. "No, nothing. As long as we're in agreement."

"We are."

"Good." He turned and left her. She watched him, resenting the feeling of disappointment that rose within her. He could seem so close. . . .

And then so damn distant. He could demand, then walk away so quickly.

She had an awful night. And she *did* have a very early morning.

She had a number of print ads to place, and she had to deal with the various stations to get the Seashell Sunblock commercial on the air. Her morning was busy enough to allow her to forget for long moments her mortification of Friday night.

But around lunchtime Janis came in and hopped up on her desk, swinging her feet. "I took a few personal messages for you from Sam when you were on the phone with the networks."

"Great, thanks. Shoot."

"Your mother. She really wants you to call her."

Kaitlin winced. "I will."

"And Donna called from Massachusetts. She said that she knew you were really busy, so she went ahead and made travel arrangements for you. She knows that you hate to fly unless it's a life-and-death situation, so you're on the morning train next Tuesday. A messenger will drop the ticket here. You've got a sleeper to New York, then—''

"Then I have to change trains. I know. Thanks, go on." She winced again. Donna was going to be a bride. She was supposed to be helping Donna. Donna shouldn't be having to make arrangements for her just to make sure she showed up.

"Barbara wanted you to remember that you're looking for gowns with her on Thursday night."

"Right."

"Your grandmother wanted you to remember that her wedding is this Saturday."

"I remember," Kaitlin said wryly.

"And . . ."

"And?"

"Your ex called."

"Brendan?"

"Do you have another ex?" Janis asked with a definite hint of mischief.

"No, I do not. What did he want?"

Janis sighed. "Whatever he wanted from me, I'd be sure to give him. Kaitlin, that is one gorgeous man. Arriving out of your past! It's so wonderful."

"It isn't wonderful at all."

Janis wasn't listening to her. She sighed again. "You know, when men appear from my past, I'm always left wondering what I was ever doing with them in the first place! They all have these huge pot bellies and have to comb their hair from one side of their heads to the other to cover up the bald spots. They never, never look like your ex-husband.''

Kaitlin smiled with an effort. ''He is a nice looking man,'' she said casually.

''Nice looking!''

''Janis...''

''All right, all right. It's just that I understand now why you don't date.''

''I do date!''

''Once a year.''

''That's ridiculous.''

''Never mind. If you're accustomed to prime rib, it's hard as heck to settle for ground chuck.''

''I'm not accustomed to anything.''

''See there—you don't date!'' Janis said triumphantly.

Kaitlin groaned. ''I am not getting anywhere with this conversation. Janis, listen closely. What did Brendan want when he called?''

''Oh—just to remind you that you've having dinner on Wednesday night.''

''Right.''

''Dinner, Kaitlin. You're dating him again! It's so romantic!''

''It's not romantic! It's—it's dinner.''

Janis nodded knowingly. ''Prime rib,'' she agreed.

''Janis!''

Janis leaped off her desk. ''I'm going. If you need me, just holler.''

"I'll holler, all right," Kaitlin promised. Janis grinned and disappeared.

The remainder of the day passed in a rush of work. She was glad of it, glad of the layouts she had to approve, glad of all the arrangements and haggling and scheduling she had to deal with. It was nearly seven when she finished, and everyone in the office had gone home except for Janis, who had waited for her.

They decided to have pizza together before going home. When Kaitlin reached her house, she showered and fell into bed, then enjoyed a completely dreamless night.

Tuesday passed quickly, too. There was still so much she had to attend to. And she made a point of calling Donna and her mother, which took a chunk out of the day, as well.

Tuesday night she had dinner with Netty Green and Garrett Harley. It was a wretched occasion with Netty endlessly praising the commercial. Kaitlin knew she should have enjoyed it. If only Netty hadn't been quite so gung-ho on Brendan.

By Wednesday she was still knee deep in reworking some of her local print ads. At five she glanced at her watch and decided that she had time left. She called Danny in and started reworking the ad for a local clothing store. She soon lost all track of time.

Then there was a tap on her office door, and she looked up. Janis quickly swept in, leaning dramatically against the desk.

"What is it?" Kaitlin asked her.

Janis grimaced. "Kaitlin, it's late."

"Yes?"

"Dinner, Kaitlin! Prime rib, remember? Well, Prime Rib is here, and he doesn't seem at all pleased that you forgot all about him!"

"Oh!" Kaitlin murmured.

The door opened again, and Brendan was there, darkly handsome in a suit, his eyes flashing, his jaw set.

"Excuse me, Ms. O'Herlihy. We did have an agreement, didn't we?"

She was a mess. Her hair was disheveled, her linen suit wrinkled, and she was certain that she had ink-stains on her hands. How could she have forgotten?

And what did she care?

"Well?"

Danny and Janis were both staring at her, seemingly enjoying her predicament. She tried to smile.

"I'm sorry, Brendan, I really did lose track of time."

He didn't say a word. She picked up her handbag and told Danny, "We'll finish in the morning, all right?"

"Sure," he said agreeably. He walked over and shook Brendan's hand. "Hi. I'm Dan Clover. It's nice to meet you, Mr. O'Herlihy."

Brendan nodded cordially. His mouth was still tight.

Kaitlin ignored his look and sailed out of the office. Brendan said good night to Danny and Janis, then followed her. Suddenly he paused, frowning.

"What's the matter?" Kaitlin asked him.

"Your friend is saying something to you," he told her.

Kaitlin walked back to the door.

"Prime Rib!" Janis whispered.

"Prime!" Danny laughed.

Kaitlin slammed the office door on both of them, irritated to discover that she was moving as quickly as she could.

Prime Rib had a temper.

Chapter 6

They were out of the office and on the street before Kaitlin paused. Then she spun around with vehemence. "Don't come into my office like that again, Brendan O'Herlihy."

"Don't stand me up again."

"I wasn't standing you up. I was just—"

"You were just biding your time, right?"

"I was busy."

"Well, Ms. O'Herlihy, I have a schedule of my own, but I do keep appointments."

Appointments! Their dinner was an appointment?

She turned, heading down the street toward her car. He came up quickly behind her, catching her arm. "I'll drive."

She jerked free from his hold. "You'll drive? I need my car. We don't live in the same place, remember?"

He released her arm suddenly. She realized then that his hair was still damp from a recent shower, his cologne was light and enticing, and he looked wonderful in a navy suit with a peach shirt beneath, emphasizing the bronzed coloring of his rugged features. She was instantly sorry, although she wasn't at all sure why. It was his fault.

"I don't think we ever *did* live together," he said softly and turned, then started walking away.

Good. She needed him out of her life. And he'd had no right to swing his temper around in her office. She hadn't been trying to ignore him or back out of anything.

Yes, she was in the right....

But she didn't want him to leave. She bit her lip, swallowed her pride and strode after him.

Damn him. His legs were long, and she had to run. Her temper started soaring again when she realized that she was running after him. She was thirty—and she was still running after Brendan O'Herlihy.

"Brendan!" Enough was enough. She stopped dead and called his name.

He stopped, too, and turned to her. So, it seemed, did half the people on the street.

"I'm sorry I was late. I really didn't do it on purpose. It's going to be difficult for me to take time off next week, and I got involved in things."

He stared at her for a long moment.

She ground her teeth together, about to turn and walk off.

Of course, his strides were longer. If he chose to catch up with her, he wouldn't have to run.

He always had the advantage, or so it seemed.

But she didn't have to turn away. He was striding toward her. "Let's just take my car for now," he told her. "I'll bring you back for yours later, and follow you home."

She mused over his suggestion. "All right," she consented at last.

He took her arm, and they started down the street. She didn't know what kind of car they were heading for, but it didn't surprise her when they reached a sleek black Mercedes sedan with a tan interior. It was a small car, comfortable, subtly elegant inside.

"Piracy must pay very well," she murmured, sinking into her seat.

He met her gaze in the mirror. "Piracy has always been a high-paying profession," he replied casually.

She fell silent as he turned the key in the ignition and drove into the traffic. He didn't speak, either, as they drove. Eventually she realized that they were heading toward her house. "You're just taking me home? I should have brought my own car."

Not until they reached her place and he had turned off the car did he lean back and look at her. "I'm sorry," he said. "And I didn't think about your car. I just thought you might want to shower and change. We can get the car later, I promise."

She smiled. "It's all right. But you know, you still have one awful temper."

"Blame it on the Irish," he murmured.

"Well, we're in the same boat there, aren't we?" she teased.

But he was studying her seriously. "You said something like that the other night," he murmured.

"Like what?"

He wasn't looking at her anymore. He was staring at the deserted street. "That we had so much in common. Ancestry, religion, ideals...you...you see so many people combat different cultures and faiths, and they make it. We had everything going for us."

"Maybe there just wasn't enough love," she said softly.

He swung around on her, his eyes very green and intense. "I don't believe that, Kaitlin. I don't believe it for a minute."

She felt suddenly trapped, as if she needed air, needed to escape. "I don't know, Brendan," she said lightly. "All I knew then was that you withdrew from me."

"I never really left you."

"You might as well have," she said softly, and before he could respond, she had opened the car door and was heading toward the house. She was suddenly very afraid of the conversation going any deeper. She didn't want him to pursue it.

Tears were stinging her eyes, and she didn't know why. It hadn't been for lack of love! she thought. Not on her part!

He followed her more slowly. She couldn't quite seem to get her key to fit properly in the lock. It finally gave just as he came up behind her. She felt his hands on her waist, his breath against her ear.

"Want to start the evening over?" There was something wonderfully warm and yet decadently provocative about the way he said the words. About the moist heat of that whisper against her earlobe. She felt that touch, and she felt his hands, and deep inside, she trembled.

She turned quickly. "You're not supposed to seduce me, Brendan."

His eyebrows shot up. "Am I that good? It was really just an innocent question."

"No, you're not that good," she lied. "I just don't want you getting any ideas."

"Sweetheart, you were the one with the ideas, remember?"

She let out a soft oath and hurried into the house. He followed, flicking on the light. She left him in the living room and headed for her bedroom, then paused, calling back, "Yes!"

"Yes, what?"

"I want to start the evening over."

"Good, we're going to have to. I'll try to postpone our dinner reservations, since we're not going to make eight-thirty by any stretch of the imagination."

She winced and called, "That's no way to start the evening over."

"Hey, it's the truth!"

"But there was a lot of sarcasm in your voice. Like it's all my fault."

"Well . . ."

"As if you're not willing to forgive."

She paused by her bedroom door. She couldn't see him, so she just waited. And then he said softly, "All right, I forgive you for being late."

She smiled. "And I forgive you for walking into my office like an avenging angel."

He didn't answer her. A second later she heard him on the phone with the restaurant where he had made their dinner reservations.

She hurried through her shower, then slipped into clean stockings and swore softly as she searched through her closet. She found an elegant black knit with subtle beadwork and a softly flaring skirt and slipped it on, then stepped into her high-heeled black pumps. She paused briefly before the mirror to do her makeup, then started to wind up her hair. After a moment, she let it fall. Brendan had always liked her hair loose.

"Stop it," she warned herself. "You're acting as if we're dating again. Again? We never really dated. We fell in love, we fell into estrangement, we fell into anger, into almost parenthood, then into distance and divorce. We never really dated. Oh, and then we had dinner once. Dinner and sex!'' Her reflection stared at her mockingly.

"No champagne, I swear. I'll drink iced tea all night!'' she vowed to her reflection.

She dumped a few things from her big leather purse into a small beaded bag and glanced at her watch. Thirty minutes. He couldn't complain.

He didn't. He was sitting on the sofa, watching a newscast, waiting for her. When she appeared, he rose quickly.

"Was I too long?'' she asked him.

He smiled slowly. Rakishly. Just like he had smiled in high school. "You're definitely worth waiting for,'' he told her. He came to stand before her and took her arm. His whisper touched her cheek, and for a moment she thought he was going to kiss her. "Very definitely,'' he said softly.

Then he turned away and opened the door for her. When they reached the car, he opened that door for her, too. Brendan had a knack for such things. She had to admit that he'd always been courteous without being patronizing. Now, leaning against the comfortable upholstery, she smiled.

"You're not a bad date,'' she told him. "Sorry—appointment.''

He cast her a dry glance. "Is this an appointment?''

"You tell me.''

"I have appointments with professors and congressmen and students and my divers. I think I want this to be a date."

"We never really dated, you know," she told him.

He flashed her another quick, amused glance. "Well, we did just about everything else, so we might as well get the dating in now, huh?"

She didn't answer him, but she could tell that he wasn't expecting an answer. And it was a nice silence that developed between them. **A c**ompanionable silence. The car had a wonderful speaker system, and soft rock rolled out from it as gracefully as the car itself rolled down the road.

The restaurant was in an old hotel in Coral Gables. It was one that Kaitlin loved. When they were seated, the maître d' handed her a rose. A waiter took her shoes, and a soft satin pillow was placed beneath her feet.

Brendan arched a skeptical brow to her when he was given the wine list. "As long as it's not champagne..." he offered.

"I'll have tea," she said primly. "Iced tea."

But he pointed out that the restaurant had half bottles of a very nice white wine, and she decided that she could manage just a little wine with dinner. Then they ordered escargot and crab cocktails, and Kaitlin decided that she just might enjoy the night.

He told her about the place he had booked for Donna's party, then he drew out the menu and handed it to her. She looked at him and sighed. "Brendan, I really don't have any right. You've been planning this—''

''I've gotten a place for the party, Kaitlin, that's all. We're in this together.''

She took the menu from him. ''Only if I get to pay for half.'' `

''Kaitlin, it's really no big thing.''

''Yes, it is! It's their shower!''

He was silent for a moment. ''When I left the beach the other day, your assistant insisted on paying me for modeling.''

Kaitlin grinned, looking at her plate. ''Brendan, we had to pay you. It would have been illegal not to.''

''Okay. Did you pay yourself?''

''Actually, yes.''

''Neither of us intended to do that commercial, right? So we'll use the money we made to pay for the party.'' He leaned back and waited for her answer.

Her smile broadened. ''Perfect!'' she told him softly. Then she bent and began to study the menu. ''This sounds wonderful.'' She laughed. ''Really wonderful! We couldn't begin to get such a nice selection for these prices down here. I'm glad Barbara wants a traditional girl thing.''

''I don't think what Joe wants is really traditional,'' he told her.

She looked up. ''Oh? What does Joe want?''

''A cruise. One of those one-day things.''

''A cruise?'' She frowned.

Brendan laughed. "He doesn't want a blonde to jump out of a cake. He just wants to gamble."

She grinned and turned her attention to the menu. She read off the appetizers, and they both decided on Donna's and Bill's favorites, then went on to the salad, the main course and dessert. She promised to make up the invitations and get them out by the next night if he could give her the guest list.

The crab cocktails disappeared, then the escargot. The chef suggested a fish delicately seasoned and cooked in a paper bag. Although Kaitlin had never really gotten used to the idea of eating a fish that still had its head intact, she felt daring and opted for it when Brendan enthusiastically endorsed it.

The fish was delicious, the wine perfect. She felt both relaxed and clearheaded. She and Brendan discussed going in together for their gifts to the various bridal couples. They toyed with several ideas, then decided that they still had time to choose.

Finally their waiter brought them espresso, and they lingered over the tiny cups.

Kaitlin idly stirred sugar into hers and found herself studying Brendan intently. He looked at her, and she quickly turned her attention to her cup. Then she looked at him again.

"Yes?" he prompted.

"I was just curious."

"About what?"

It sometimes seemed that he hadn't changed at all, that things hadn't changed. He'd barely walked back into her life, yet it almost seemed as if he'd never been out of it. But he had. There were eons between them, yet it seemed that he had never really been very far away.

"You have your house in the Keys," she said.

He shrugged. "Yes."

"But you must go home often enough. You're still such good friends with Bill that he wants you to be his best man."

"I keep a house in Massachusetts, too," he told her.

"In the Worcester area?"

He shook his head. "I have a place in the country. Out by Orange, almost on the New Hampshire border. I have about twenty acres there."

She was staring at him blankly.

"Is that all right with you?" he asked.

She gave herself a little shake. Of course. It was fine. It was just that no one had ever told her.

Well, she had said once that she didn't want to hear about Brendan O'Herlihy. And it seemed that all her family and friends had taken her words to heart.

"Of course it's all right. I guess I had just been wondering... what you'd been up to all these years."

"Piracy, remember?"

She nodded. "Yes, right." She was silent for a moment. "And I take it that you've seen a lot of Barbara and Joe over the years, too."

"Obviously. You know that."

"You come up from the Keys very often?"

He hesitated for a moment, then shrugged again. "Sure. I need to go by the research facilities at the university now and then. And I take students out for dives. I have a lot of colleagues who are professors. I keep an apartment on Brickell."

Brickell! It was right down the street from her office.

And Barbara had known all along, but never said a word to her.

"How long have you had the apartment?" she asked stiffly.

"About two years."

"And they all knew..." she muttered beneath her breath.

He made an impatient sound. "Kaitlin, you've known that Joe and I kept up. And that meant that Barbara and I did, too."

"I didn't know how much. I knew that Joe knew where you were, since he told me where to find you when—"

"When you came down to offer me your... bargain."

"I didn't come down to bargain."

"What *were* you doing, then?"

"I came in an effort to make things easier for both of us."

"Like hell!"

"I wasn't seeing anyone seriously at the time."

"Well," he mused, his green gaze bright as he leaned back in his chair, studying her broadly, "I'm glad to hear that."

"What—"

"I'm glad you weren't deeply involved with another man while you were bargaining with me."

"Brendan, how can you make it all sound so—so decadent!"

"Because it was," he said flatly.

"I lead the life of a cloistered nun—" she began furiously, then broke off, aware of just how much she was giving away about her own life.

"What?"

"Nothing! I wasn't bargaining with you!"

"Well, you did fall into bed with me rather easily. I'm glad that you weren't contemplating another marriage at the time."

She gasped, her temper rising. "Damn you, Brendan. Maybe I fell into bed easily with you, but you fell into bed with me easily, too!"

He didn't reply for an instant. Then he said, very softly, "But I wasn't asking you for an annulment." She suddenly sensed that he was looking behind her rather than at her.

She twisted around to see that their waiter, his face an impossible shade of crimson, discreetly attempting to give Brendan the check.

She felt the blood rush to her face as she recalled the last few lines of their conversation. She wanted to explode, to sink beneath the table. . . .

Or tear out every ebony hair in Brendan's head. The silver ones, too.

She stood, grabbing her handbag. "Thank you for dinner," she said stiffly, then hurried blindly out of the restaurant.

She had barely made it through the front door, though, when he came striding up behind her, catching her arm and swinging her around.

"What do you think you're doing?" he demanded.

"Going home. I'll get a cab—"

"The hell you will."

"I'll do—"

"You came out with me tonight, Kaitlin. You'll damn well go home with me, too."

His hand was on her elbow. She gritted her teeth, looking down the street. There wasn't a cab in sight, and there wasn't likely to be. Not at this time of night, in such a quiet area.

He started walking toward his car, with her following slowly, digging her heels in stubbornly. He opened the door for her. "Will you get in, please? And quit being so mad at me because the waiter heard you talking about your sex life—or lack thereof."

Her eyes flew to his with renewed fury. "You son of a—"

"Kaitlin, it's late. Get in."

She did so only because she had no choice. He quickly walked around and slid into the driver's seat, then revved the engine. After he had pulled onto the street, he met her eyes.

"If you weren't seeing anyone, why did you want the annulment?"

She shook her head, unwilling to explain.

"Why?"

She lifted her hands vaguely. "My parents had mentioned a cousin who was married again. The right way. In—"

"The right way!" he exploded, his green eyes dark and shadowed and angry in the night. "What is the right way to be married, Kaitlin? Is it still only real to you if there are a million guests and you wear a dress worth a few thousand bucks? Is that it?"

She gasped, furious. "No, that is not it! The right way is the way that any individual deems to be important! For me that means in the church. For others it may be different. And it doesn't matter in the least what the hell anyone wears, or who attends. It's in the heart, Brendan, it's—oh, never mind!"

"You're damn right I'll never mind. However the hell it was done, Kaitlin, we were married. Man and wife. And we were expecting a child, and we lost that child. And I'll never pretend that it didn't happen. I'll never sign any piece of paper that says it didn't. So get that straight right now."

"I got it straight!"

He pulled over to the curb abruptly. She was suddenly afraid of his temper, wondering what he was doing. Then she realized that they were in front of her house. He got out of the car. She knew that he was going to come around and open her door, so she leaped out hastily, unwilling to have him come too close.

"Thank you for dinner!" she snapped.

"Oh, no, we're not done yet."

"Yes, we are. I wouldn't dream of asking you in. That might be construed as bargaining!"

"Kaitlin—"

"Go to hell, Brendan!"

She headed for the front door. She strode up the walkway in a searing temper, but as soon as she reached the door, she remembered that her car was still parked by the office.

She turned. Brendan was waiting for her to remember. He was leaning against the passenger door, looking superior.

She strode down the walk. "You knew all along that my car was still at the office," she snapped. "So why did you drive me here?"

"I didn't know all along. I remembered right after you went flouncing out of the car."

"I do not flounce, Brendan O'Herlihy. And I don't appreciate—"

"Kaitlin, let's go get your car."

"I can get a cab in the morning, thank you."

He shrugged. "Suit yourself. It will only take us ten minutes to go back. And taking a cab in the morning isn't going to change the fact that you will be seeing me again."

"Yes, but I'll have a few days' grace," she said sweetly.

"Not so many. Your grandmother invited me to her wedding, you know."

"Yes, I assumed that Gram would do something like that."

"I have to go."

"I imagine."

"And I really should be your escort."

Her mouth fell open. "What?"

"Do you have a date for her wedding?"

"I don't need a date!"

He smiled. "All right, then, an escort."

"If I wanted an escort, Brendan, I would get one."

His smile deepened. For a moment he looked at the ground, his dark lashes sweeping over his eyes. "You still sound like the very proud young woman I met all those years ago. Kaitlin, I know that you can get a date. You can get what you want from almost anyone just by opening those baby blues and batting an eyelash or two."

"Brendan—"

"Get in. I'll take you to get your car."

She hesitated. He stepped away and opened the door for her. She got in.

He was silent as he drove through the quiet night streets to reach her car. He parked behind it, got out and walked her over to it.

"I'll follow you home," he told her.

"It isn't necessary," she said stiffly.

"It is to me."

She got into her car and started it.

Yet as she drove home, she saw that he had followed her, and that he was following her all the way.

She parked in her driveway. When she got out, he was leaning against his car once again, watching as she headed up the walk, fitted her key into the lock and turned to wave.

"I'm home. Safely," she said.

He nodded. "Call me if you change your mind about Saturday. We could use the practice."

"For what?"

"Weddings," he called back. "We've got two to attend together."

"I won't change my mind," she said sweetly.

He chuckled softly. "Call me if you do. But not too late. I might pull a date out of a hat myself."

She didn't answer as she stepped into the house, then closed and locked the door.

She stripped off her clothing and donned a nightgown quickly. She was exhausted.

But she didn't sleep. She wondered what Brendan did with his time when he wasn't working. She had told him that she wasn't seriously involved.

She had told him that she lived like a nun!

She sighed and tossed around, and tried again to sleep. When she finally dozed, she was beset by dreams.

Of Brendan. And in her dreams, he was curled up beside her; they were naked, and he was holding her close.

In her dream they were married again. Sleeping together, entwined. His chin was resting on the top of her head, and she was comfortable and secure....

She woke with a start. It was still the middle of the night. She rose and hurried into the kitchen, where she made a cup of tea.

As she sat sipping it, she realized that she had never remarried because she had not met anyone who could make her feel the way that Brendan did.

But it was always so painful when they were together! Their tempers flared, and their words were bitter. But there was so much more, so much they never said. The words wouldn't come, so the bitterness remained.

She stayed awake for a while, then she made herself go back to bed.

The next day was insane from start to finish.

She had work to do, and more. After work she had to check dinner arrangements with Gram, then they had to check on the cake.

Next she had to meet with Barbara, and they went from shop to shop to shop trying to find the perfect gown.

At the sixth place, they found it at last.

The gown was stunning. The satin bodice and low-cut back were enhanced by a soft mesh that covered Barbara's back and collarbone, ending in a slim row of pearls below her throat. A small teardrop pearl sat where the satin met the gauze at the cleft of her breasts.

The train was exquisite, long, beaded and sequined. And the gown fit Barbara perfectly.

"It's stunning!" Kaitlin told her. Watching Barbara, she felt tears well in her eyes. Her cousin was so beautiful. And she had waited so long to be a bride.

"Will Joe like it?" Barbara asked anxiously.

"He'll love it!" Kaitlin promised her. "Oh, Barbara! It's perfect!"

So Barbara left a down payment on the gown, and then they looked at dresses for the bridesmaids, deciding on black and white gowns. They were wonderful, too, with black velvet bodices and beautiful white skirts.

That done, they went and had dinner and a drink. Barbara had a champagne cocktail, and Kaitlin carefully chose a white wine spritzer. She was relieved that Barbara didn't mention Brendan.

By the time Kaitlin reached home, she was too tired to think, or even to dream.

The next afternoon her parents arrived. She picked them up at the airport, and as soon as she saw them, she was besieged with guilt.

They were wonderful. Her mother was a younger version of Gram, an older version of herself. She had flawless skin and beautiful blue eyes, and though she looked like a woman of fifty, she was a very, very lovely fifty. She was dressed smartly, and she walked with her arm linked through Kaitlin's father's.

Her dad was great, too. A very tall, gray-haired man with steely gray eyes and strong, handsome features.

They'd been married since they were twenty, and they had obviously never fallen out of love. Kaitlin was an only child simply because there hadn't been any others, even though her mother would have liked a houseful. She was the one object of their affection, and they were very loving, yet careful never to smother her.

They deserve so much more than I give them! Kaitlin thought. And having located them in the crowd, she suddenly tore through the mob to reach them.

"Mom! Dad!" She hugged them both enthusiastically, not at all sure why her eyes were suddenly so wet.

"Kaitlin!" Her mother hugged her, then she was in her father's arms. He held her very close, then he released her slowly.

"Sweetheart, it's so good to see you!"

She nodded. "Let's get out of here. It's a zoo!"

She linked arms with them both and led them to her car. She chatted all the while about the wedding plans, and her mother told her who was going to be able to make it down.

"Donna wanted to come, and so did Patrick." Patrick was Donna's older brother. "But Patrick's wife is having a baby, and she hasn't been very well, so she's been in and out of the hospital. Donna's been taking care of Brandy, and they didn't make up that saying about the terrible twos for nothing!"

Kaitlin felt a pang of guilt. She was supposed to be helping Donna, and she hadn't even known that Donna was taking care of her nephew. "Maybe I can help when I come up next week," she said.

"Don't miss your train, young lady," her father warned her.

She smiled. "I won't, Dad. I promise."

"It's too bad you don't like to fly," he said.

"I hate to fly—unless I absolutely have to," she admitted.

"Maybe it's good for you to take trains, anyway," her father said shrewdly. "You relax a bit, at least."

Her mother frowned slightly, warning her dad not to tread on her private concerns. "So tell me about Mr. Rosen!" she said.

Kaitlin smiled and did so. They reached her car and drove to her house, and the conversation didn't lull once. Once they arrived, Kaitlin heated some soup she had made, while her mother and father settled into the guest room. Her dad was the first one into the kitchen. He tasted the soup, winked and told her it was terrific.

"So how is everything with you?" he asked her.

"Great, Dad. The agency is really holding its own."

"I'm proud of you, you know."

She hugged him again just because she loved him so much. She knew it was hard for him that she lived fifteen hundred miles away from home.

"I've spent my whole life being proud of you, you know," she told him.

"Thanks," he said huskily. He leaned against the counter and asked about her work.

She told him that they'd just brought in a really big account. She didn't tell him that she'd participated in her own commercial. With Brendan.

He listened, commenting on her minor problems. Then he asked her, "What about you?"

"About me?"

"Are you happy, Kaitlin?"

"Oh! Well, of course, I'm happy."

"Are you seeing anyone?"

She turned to the soup. "I've been really busy lately."

"You're not seeing anyone at all?"

It was her mother's dismayed voice that she heard, and she turned and smiled. "Mom, I do see people. Really."

"Will we meet anyone at Gram's wedding?" she asked anxiously.

Now it was her father's turn to frown at her mother, who ignored him.

"Well, not at Gram's wedding." They were both staring at her. "I've been so busy. I'm her maid of honor, you know, Mom." They were still staring at her. "I won't be there alone. I couldn't really bring anyone because...well, she asked Brendan. So I thought that I really should let him escort me."

Her father's jaw dropped; her mother beamed. "Brendan? I knew that he'd be Bill's best man, but he's here? Now? And we'll see him at Gram's wedding?''

Kaitlin wondered with a certain annoyance if her parents weren't more excited about seeing Brendan than they were about seeing their own daughter.

Then she felt guilty.

She turned to the soup again. Damn you, Brendan! she thought furiously. Then she realized in a small panic that she needed to call him and let him know that she needed a **date** after all.

Whatever had possessed her to say anything to her parents? It had been the way they looked at her, so anxiously....

She managed to steer the conversation away from him during dinner. And at least her parents made it an early night.

As soon as they were in bed, she closed herself into her own room. She called information, only to learn that Brendan's number was unlisted. Then she swallowed hard, bit the proverbial bullet and called Joe.

She ignored the curious tone of his voice, got Brendan's number and called him quickly, before she could chicken out.

He took forever to answer! She closed her eyes and wondered what he was doing. His apartment might well be an impressive bachelor pad, with a Jacuzzi on the balcony. And he might already be working on a date. She'd be dark. Very dark, and very sexy...

"Hello?"

She moistened her lips. She couldn't speak.

"Hello?" he repeated with annoyance. She knew Brendan; he wouldn't stay on the line long.

Her fingers wound around the phone cord. "Brendan, it's me. Kaitlin. O'Herlihy," she added inanely, and winced.

"O'Herlihy, eh?" he said, and she heard a trace of amusement in his tone. "And what can I do for you, Ms. O'Herlihy?"

"I need you. I mean, I don't need you. I want you—no, no, that's not what I mean."

"Just what *do* you mean?"

"I've changed my mind. About the wedding. Gram's. That is, if you haven't already gotten another date."

He was silent for so long that she began to wish she had never called. She was ready to slam the receiver down when she heard him speak again, his voice husky and deep.

"No, I haven't made any other arrangements. I'd be delighted to escort you, Ms. O'Herlihy. What time shall you require my services?"

Chapter 7

It was really a beautiful wedding.

Gram and Al Rosen were married beneath a flowered trellis in a courtyard. It was a simple ceremony, but the two of them had written their own vows, which were very traditional. They promised to love, honor and cherish each other for all the time that God should grant them, until death should them part.

Standing by her grandmother's side, Kaitlin felt tears welling in her eyes. She thought honesty was the only thing that mattered between two people. Gram and Al were both so sure of what they were doing. And their love was evident to everyone present.

For a small wedding, it was a surprisingly large affair. Donna and her brother hadn't been able to make it, but their folks were there. All four of Gram's daughters—Maeve, Kaitlin's mother; Margaret, Donna's mother; Bede, Barbara's mother; and Siobhan, their youngest sister—were there. Gram's sons, Galen and Michael, were there, too, with their wives. And there were seven cousins, counting her and Barbara—Michael, Jeremy, Joshua, Liam and Catherine Mary. Al Rosen had a big family, too, and many of them were in attendance. And then there were Gram's and Mr. Rosen's friends, the oldest and spryest gentleman being an old friend of Al's father, a Timothy Tyron.

After the bride and groom had been on the dance floor for a few minutes, Al's best man, his son Jacob, brought Kaitlin out to the floor. Then everyone joined in, and Brendan cut in on Jacob to take Kaitlin into his arms.

"How are you holding up?" he asked her.

"Fine, thanks."

"Your parents look good."

She nodded.

"They're beaming at us."

"They like to believe in miracles."

He grinned. "It hurt like hell to call me, huh?"

"It wasn't easy," she admitted. And it hadn't gotten any easier. Her parents had been glad to see Brendan, and she'd discovered that even her mother and father had seen him occasionally over the years without mentioning the fact to her. And he looked great. He had picked her up in a blue suit with very thin pinstripes and a handsome vest. The magnificent cut of the suit enhanced his hard physique, his muscled shoulders, his lean hips. And he smelled great, too. She hated it when he was this appealing. It was hard enough to be with him to begin with. They had grown so far apart, yet so many thing felt so familiar.

"It's a beautiful wedding," he murmured softly. "Your grandmother is a very classy lady."

Kaitlin had to smile. "She is."

"She's in love with him. She's going through the paces, but you can tell that the music, the trappings, none of that really matters. He's the only thing that matters to her."

She looked at him. Was he implying again that all she had ever wanted were the trappings?

"Brendan, don't—"

"You know, I still remember meeting you. Seeing your eyes. The challenge, the determination. I don't think I'd ever seen anything as beautiful, as captivating, as your face."

His eyes were on her, and his body was close, brushing hers, hot against hers, as they moved. She wanted to tear herself away; she was breathless and afraid. There was too much history between them. He had not only broken her heart, he had stamped on it. And then he had humiliated her. If only he wasn't looking at her so...

The song was over, but they were still standing there in each other's arms. Then the band began to play something else, and Brendan moved to the faster tempo. As Kaitlin followed his lead, she realized that a majority of her family was watching her. And she knew that they were all thinking she had been a fool, that it was her fault she was no longer married to Brendan O'Herlihy.

"Remember the good old days, Kaitlin?" he asked lightly.

"I remember that you left me," she told him defensively.

He shook his head. "I never left you."

"You ran off and joined the Navy. I call that leaving me."

"I thought you wanted to be with someone else."

Then her father was there, cutting in on Brendan, and she was swept away again. She tried to smile, tried to act delighted, tried to chat and laugh. But she knew she was failing dismally, and her father knew, too, but he didn't let on.

"Brendan looks good," he told her.

"Brendan always looks good," she said wearily. "And he's smart, and he's successful, and I was the biggest fool on earth to file those papers."

Her dad frowned. "Kaitlin, what—"

"I can tell. I can see it in everyone's eyes. I come out the heavy."

"Honey, there is no heavy in a situation like that."

"Dad, no one could understand. No one who didn't know him like I did. Sean died, and a piece of Brendan died, too. He was there after that, but he was never with me."

"Kaitlin, no one is blaming you."

"I wish he'd fall on his face."

Her dad laughed. "That's bitter. It doesn't sound like you."

"Well, I am bitter." She was silent for a minute. "I don't really want anything bad to happen to him. I just want all his hair to fall out and his weight to balloon. Maybe a blackened tooth or two would help."

Her father laughed and swung her around. "Sounds to me like you're still in love."

She shook her head vehemently. "No, Dad, never. It hurts too much."

He was serious. "Remember Sean, honey? I do. And that was something that he always saw. There has to be discord for us to know harmony. Pain so we can feel pleasure. Tragedy so there can be comedy."

"I remember Sean," she murmured. He had been right, of course. But he had never warned her that the pain could go on for years and years and years.

Then Al Rosen cut in, and her father had no choice but to release her.

Then she was needed by the maître d'. There were too many people for the present seating arrangements. Desperate, she rearranged everything, careful not to offend Mr. Rosen's family or her own.

By the time she finished, she felt exhausted, frazzled. And when she came out, she found out that she had forgotten about one very major guest—Al's rabbi. She hurried back and started over. Thank God for the band. They kept playing and playing.

Finally things were set and the guests could pick up their table numbers.

She danced with her uncles and with her cousins. And with her new step-grandfather. Even when the meal was served, she barely saw Brendan.

Then the band struck up again, and she had a moment to herself when she leaned against the wall and fanned herself, laughing as Gram tossed her bouquet—and Barbara caught it. Then Al Rosen slipped off Gram's garter and managed to toss it to Joe, who made quite a production of getting it onto Barbara's leg.

Then there was more dancing. From her vantage point Kaitlin could see that Timothy Tyron was keeping pace with all the activity. He was definitely in the swing of things. He didn't care whether the band was playing the hora or a waltz or an Irish jig, he was right in the middle of it.

After a while she was called into the bride's room, because the gifts were overflowing the tables that had been set up for them. While she was looking for a busboy to help her carry things to various cars, she suddenly heard a loud scream, then numerous shouts and absolute chaos.

She came running out and saw a large crowd around the dance floor.

"An ambulance!" someone shouted.

"It's been called!"

Then another voice, smooth and authoritative, warned everyone to get back. Kaitlin didn't know what was going on, but her heart was in her throat.

Gram!

Where was her grandmother? She wanted to worry about Al Rosen, but she couldn't change the fact that she had been blessed with a grandmother for thirty years, and Al was still a stranger.

"What's happened?" she shouted.

Then an arm slipped through hers. Her father was at her side, and she looked up at him with wide, terrified eyes. "Gram!"

He shook his head. She could hear the ambulance siren wailing. "Gram is fine," her father told her. "It's that nice old Timothy Tyron. I think he danced a bit too much."

"Oh!" she cried.

Then the ambulance was there, and the paramedics were coming through, carrying a stretcher.

Yet even as they did, Timothy Tyron was opening his eyes, his hand held by none other than Brendan O'Herlihy. Then the crowd closed in again, cheering and applauding as Timothy was helped onto the stretcher. He was still gripping Brendan's hand, and Al was walking at his other side. "It was that last hora, I think," Timothy said.

"You'll be up and about soon," Al promised him.

Timothy grinned and closed his eyes while the paramedics managed to get an oxygen mask on him.

Then Kaitlin stared after the stretcher and the departing backs of Al, Brendan and the attendants.

"What happened?" she whispered.

Her cousin Michael was behind her. "He fainted, I think. It's a good thing Brendan was around, or the old guy might have breathed his last."

"Brendan!" Kaitlin exclaimed.

"Somehow Timothy stopped breathing, but Brendan got him started again."

"Oh," Kaitlin murmured, so glad that Timothy was going to be okay.

And she didn't know why she resented the fact that Brendan had been the big hero of the day.

Al came in, announcing that Timothy seemed to be doing well. There was more cheering, but the party was winding down.

Gram found Kaitlin and gave her a big kiss and a teary-eyed thank you. Then she kissed the rest of her family, and she and Al departed for their honeymoon.

There was more dancing, but soon the guests began to drift away.

Kaitlin felt that the responsibility of holding down the fort until the very end was hers, so she said goodbye to the last of the guests, then slipped off her shoes and collapsed into a chair at one of the tables. Her parents were beside her, and she knew that Brendan was behind her, waiting.

Politely, the perfect escort.

The hero of the whole affair.

Why was she so resentful? Or was it just that she was tired?

"I think that's the end of it," Brendan murmured. "I'll get the car and meet you out front."

She nodded without looking at him. Her mother thanked him. Kaitlin wasn't sure if she was glad her parents were there, or if she just wished that she could be alone with him to tell him . . .

Tell him what?

She wanted to scream at him, to smash her fists against his chest. And she wasn't even sure why.

"Tired?" her mother asked her softly.

"Exhausted."

"And you've got two to go," Maeve reminded her.

"But it's fun, it's great—"

"And exhausting," her dad said, laughing.

"Everything was perfect except for poor Mr. Tyron," Kaitlin said.

"Let me warn you, Kaitlin," her dad said. "There's always some little trauma at a wedding."

"I'm not going to allow any more little traumas," she said firmly. And when her parents exchanged amused glances, she insisted, "I'm not!"

Neither of them corrected her. They had reached the door, and Brendan was there with the car. Kaitlin's dad opened the door for her and her mother, and Kaitlin slid into the seat next to Brendan.

And then she didn't know what happened.

Suddenly Brendan was waking her up. She blinked furiously as she realized that she was sleeping with her head on his lap, and they were parked in front of her house.

"Kaitlin, your parents have already gone in."

"Oh. Oh!" Her fingers were curled around his thigh. She felt his warmth, the slight movement of a muscle.

She jerked upright.

"Let me help you—"

"No. No, please, I'm awake. I'm going in. I—thank you. I do appreciate you serving as my escort," she said coldly.

She started to slide out of the car, but he caught her arm and pulled her back. Despite the darkness, she could see the glitter in his eyes. "If you're so damn appreciative, why are you being so rude?"

"I'm not. I'm just tired."

"I'll walk you to the door."

"No! It's all right!"

But he was already out of the car and coming around to open her door. She jumped out quickly, not wanting to give him an excuse to touch her.

"What the hell is the matter with you?" he demanded.

"Nothing. I don't know." She backed away from him. "I just—I just think we need to put a little distance between us."

"Kaitlin, we've got years of distance."

"Right. Well, thank you, good night."

His jaw twisted. "You know, Kaitlin, once, just once, I'd love to hear from you when you didn't want something."

"You said to call you—"

"You called me because your family was here. Because you didn't feel like dredging up a date who meant nothing to you. A date who would expect to be entertained like any other guest."

"What difference does it make?" she demanded.

He came close, threading his fingers into her hair and pulling her against him before she could protest. "A lot, Kaitlin. It makes a lot of difference to me."

"We're not all perfect like you," she said.

"Like me? You think I'm perfect?"

"Always. The perfect damn hero."

"You're mad at me over Mr. Tyron!" he said incredulously.

"I'm not!" she gasped, horrified. "My God, I wouldn't want anything to happen to anyone—"

"But you wish someone else had seen to him, right?"

She was stubbornly silent.

"Kaitlin, it's part of what I do! I have to know emergency medical procedures. I have divers who get injured. Things go wrong."

"I'm not mad! I'm delighted that you could help. I'm just—"

"Just what?"

"Sick of you being so damn perfect," she muttered.

His hold tightened, and she thought he was going to kiss her. And though she was angry and confused, she wanted that kiss. She wanted the fierce heat of his lips. She wanted to taste the anger and the passion, and she wanted to let it rise and simmer and explode....

But he didn't kiss her. He released her. "Good night, Kaitlin. I guess I'll see you in Massachusetts."

"Right," she murmured. "In Massachusetts."

He opened her door and waited for her to go inside. She did, then closed the door and locked it.

Her mother and father had apparently gone to bed, because the house was dark.

She sank slowly into the couch. Her cheeks were damp, and she touched them, amazed to realize that she was crying.

And she didn't even know why.

She was afraid, she realized. Afraid of taking a chance, afraid of reaching out.

And yet she wanted Brendan. She wanted to talk to him, to make love with him. She wanted to lay her head against his shoulder and cry for the past.

And maybe find a future.

When Brendan dropped Kaitlin and her parents off, he didn't feel like returning to his apartment. It was a nice place, but it felt cramped to him. It felt like the city. It was late, but the Upper Keys weren't very far away; his house was only an hour and forty-five minutes from Kaitlin's place.

But when he reached his place in the Keys, he knew that that wasn't really where he wanted to be, either. He wanted the water, he realized.

He changed his suit for jeans and a T-shirt, then walked to the dock. His yacht, the *Lilliputian*, was gently rocking in her berth.

He hopped aboard. He knew he wasn't going anywhere; he just wanted to sit on the open deck and smell the sea breeze.

The yacht was a fine piece of craftsmanship. The woodwork was beautiful, the two staterooms were great, and even the smaller crew cabins were nice. She was equipped with all the latest in sonar devices for underwater discovery, and she could carry all the diving gear and paraphernalia he needed. When he had a big find he had to call out the heavy-duty salvage vessels, but the *Lilliputian* was the perfect vessel for discovery. There was nowhere he would rather be.

He went down the steps to the main cabin and headed to the galley for a beer, then went on deck, popped the top, sat down, leaned back and looked up at the stars. It was a beautiful night. It had been a great night for Lizzie Boyle's wedding.

"To you, Lizzie," he said softly, lifting his can. Few women were so wise, he thought. She was a very great lady.

And she was what Kaitlin would be, he thought, years and years from now.

He wished suddenly that she was here with him. It seemed that they were always fighting when they were together. They would just start to get close to the truth, then they would erupt in some argument, and the things that should have been said were left unvoiced.

If only she was here now...

But she wasn't.

He closed his eyes and felt the air move over him. It was soothing, but not soothing enough to wash away the past. He'd led such a great life in so many ways. Nice parents who supported him. Things always seemed to fall his way. He was naturally athletic, and good at academics, too. His grandparents had been Irish immigrants, just like Kaitlin's. They had believed deeply in the American dream and tried hard to give their children everything they'd never had. His grandfather had gone over history with him, then geography, and once Brendan found the oceans of the world, his dream had been born.

Best of all, he'd had Kaitlin. The most beautiful and exquisite creature he had ever seen, with her soft blue eyes and radiant hair, her pride, her laughter and her passion. No one could have asked for more, but he had more anyway. His cousin Sean.

Sean O'Herlihy had been an actor. From kindergarten on, it had seemed that Sean knew his dream. He could read circles around the rest of the family by second grade. He studied literature, and he studied plays. He loved the great Irish playwrights. He wanted one day to perform at the Abbey Theatre in Dublin, but he wanted to act on Broadway, too.

By their senior year, Sean was the hero of the high school. He played MacBeth, Romeo, anything of Shakespeare's. He produced and directed and starred in Behan's *Hostage*. He was offered several prestigious scholarships, a role on a soap opera and bit movie parts. He could mimic any accent, but his Irish was naturally the best.

For eighteen years, they had been more than cousins. They had been best friends.

Brendan would never forget the last time he'd seen Sean alive. They'd gone to the park in Rutland, just to walk. School was over; it was almost time to say goodbye. Not forever—just to the old way of life. Within a month Brendan and Kaitlin would be married and headed south, and Sean would be off on his own, headed for school in New York. Sean was enthusiastic about the bachelor party he was planning. When Brendan assured him that he was really far past the need for a blonde to jump out of a cake, Sean laughed.

"Aye, sure and begorrah!" he said and leaped atop a rock. Then he rested his chin in his hands and sighed. "No girls out of cakes, Brendan. I couldn't find one to compare with Kaitlin, anyway. You're a lucky man, you know. She's the most beautiful girl I've ever seen, and bright and sweet to boot. And I can't wait for the wedding. It will be solemn and regal and wonderful, and then it will be time to party, party, party!"

Brendan laughed and sat across from him on another boulder. "Party time, all right. We're going to be married. It's what I want more than anything, and sometimes I still can't believe it's really going to happen.''

''Believe it, my boy,'' Sean told him; then his handsome, freckled face went serious. ''Brendan, it gives me goose bumps just thinking about it. I'm going to be your best man. I can't wait. I think I'm more excited than either of you. And I love her, Brendan, you know that. I feel like she's my relative already. You're lucky. You've got love. When you've got love, you've got everything.''

''Yeah, I know.''

And they had sat there on those boulders, then skipped rocks across the creek the way they had done when they were kids. They had talked about their plans, their dreams. And they had promised that they would always come home.

''I think home for you is going to be any patch of salt water,'' Sean told Brendan.

''And home for you is going to be any stage, with the footlights shining on you.''

'' 'All the world's a stage!' '' Sean quoted. ''Sometimes comedy, and sometimes tragedy. But you've got to have the tragedy, you know. Otherwise there couldn't be heights of the ridiculous and the sublime, right?''

''Right.''

They gripped hands suddenly. ''We'll always be blood,'' Sean vowed, grinning. ''Sharing dreams.''

"Always blood," Brendan agreed. "Sharing dreams."

But there would be no more dreams for them to share. The next week his mother had come by the dive shop where he was working for the summer. There were tears in her eyes, and it was the middle of the day, and right away he knew that something was terribly wrong.

Sean was dead. He had been hit by a truck driver and killed instantly.

Brendan had never cried like that before in his life. And there was more. There was the funeral. Sean, always so full of life, lay there cold and silent and still, and he wasn't Sean anymore.

After that, nothing seemed right. If Sean was dead, then he shouldn't be alive. He shouldn't be able to feel the breeze, to see the sun, to smell the flowers.

Or Kaitlin's perfume. Or touch her, or feel the softness of her hair sweep around him. When the first stunned agony faded, he became numb, and no one could touch him. He didn't want to be touched. Nothing in his life had prepared him for losing Sean. He tried to understand that his aunt and his uncle and his other cousins were in the same pain, and he tried to understand that Kaitlin had loved Sean just as Sean had loved Kaitlin.

But he had known that he couldn't go through with the wedding. No one expected them to marry as planned, anyway. Not so soon. Sean's death was an incredible loss to both families, and everyone was going to have to struggle to go on.

But Brendan never quite got over it. When he talked to Kaitlin, he wanted to reach out to her. He wanted to drown in her whispers, in her tears, in her touch. He wanted to make love until he could feel nothing but the sweet ecstasy that would take him away, but he couldn't go near her.

Because he shouldn't be able to feel. Sean was dead. Sean would never feel again.

Brendan tried to bring himself back to her. But he still couldn't stand the idea of a wedding. Because Sean should have been at the wedding. Should have been standing beside them.

In the end Brendan had lost Kaitlin, too. She was still with him, but he had lost her. Two years passed, and they were still together. Studying, learning, leaving high school far behind them, becoming adults. And planning a wedding again. Or, at least, he kept quiet while Kaitlin planned it.

And then he found her laughing in the arms of a friend. His friend.

He had exploded and left. The next thing he knew, he had signed up for the Navy and was knee-deep in basic training.

And wishing he could go back. Once he was away from her, he knew how deeply he loved her.

The service didn't leave a guy much time for apologies. And he didn't know what to say, anyway. Then he had heard from her. A very stiff and stilted letter, telling him that she felt obliged to let him know that she was expecting a child. He needn't feel obligated to do anything about it.

He'd been able to come back then, feeling guilty, because he was thrilled. He had Kaitlin back. As his wife. And he was going to have a child, along with all the love he had discovered, nearly too late, that he needed so badly, the love that had sustained him. Quiet, undemanding, always there for him.

Then Kaitlin had lost the baby, but the news hadn't reached him until he was in the middle of the Persian Gulf.

He'd wanted to be with her. He'd wanted to be with her so badly that it ate at his insides, but by the time the news reached him, she was already out of the hospital and he had months at sea ahead of him.

By the time he returned home, Kaitlin was distant. Untouchable. And in his heart he knew long before he received the official papers that she had withdrawn herself from him.

He had been twenty-two at the time. With nothing left except his pride.

"The stuff that goeth before a fall," he reminded himself out loud. He finished his beer, staring at the stars. He thought of the years since then and the women who had passed through his life. The ones who had cared, the ones who had been casual.

He'd never been more than casual himself. He had never managed to fall out of love.

"And I still love you, Kaitlin," he whispered softly to the darkness.

But how the hell did you start over after a past like theirs?

He had missed Sean so badly. It seemed an ironic shame that it had taken him all these years to understand what his cousin had known all along. Life was a mixture of laughter and of tears. And you were just lucky if you could be loved through them both.

Once upon a time, he had had a love that strong.

And now he wanted it back.

He sat for a minute, then smiled slowly and closed his eyes against the night breeze.

Thank God for all these weddings. He was going to have a chance to try to have it all one more time.

He was older and wiser, and this time he knew that love was everything. When it was offered, you had to reach for it, and grab it, then hold it tight, through the laughter and the tears.

Yes, love was everything. . . .

Kaitlin was everything.

And he would have the chance to spend a lot more time with her next week.

With that thought in mind, he rose, threw his beer can away and patted the *Lilliputian* good night for the evening.

He was whistling as he headed to the house.

Chapter 8

Kaitlin arrived at the train station in a state of confusion.

Her parents had left just yesterday morning, she'd survived a meeting with Harley and Netty of Seashell Sunblock that afternoon, and then this morning she'd overslept, her taxi had gotten lost, and she had been afraid, what with the early morning traffic, that she was never going to reach her destination.

She did make it in time. Eight minutes before the train was due to leave.

She couldn't wait to get on board. Into a small sleeper, alone. She could read, or sleep, or relax. Actually, she could even work, but the idea of relaxing, of grouping her forces, seemed too sweet. She didn't need to work. Janis was on the job. Harley was as pleased with the finished commercial as his sister was, and the ad was already scheduled to air.

The doors to the train were open, and she trailed her wheeled baggage cart behind her as she hurried along. The conductor pointed out her car. When she reached it, the attendant helped her with her luggage, then took her ticket.

"O'Herlihy," he muttered. He was a young man with sandy hair and light freckles. He flipped his reservation chart over and muttered her name again.

"You're traveling alone?"

"Yes."

"Okay... let's see. What's your first initial?"

"K. For Kaitlin," she told him.

He shook his head again. "How unusual."

"What's the matter?"

"Oh, nothing. Really." He smiled cheerfully.

"Is there some problem?"

"Problem? No! Well, let's see, we'll try cabin A," he told her.

He moved along the narrow hallway and opened a door. The cabin was empty, and he smiled broadly. "A it is!"

"Was there something wrong with my reservation?" Kaitlin asked him.

"No. Come on in, and I'll show you the cabin. This sleeping car is one of our newest."

He said it with such pride that Kaitlin didn't dare comment on the very tiny size of the room.

"That's the top bunk up there, folded into the wall. And there's plenty of storage space above it. The seats are pulled down—I'll make up the bed for you to-night—and there's your sink." She could see the sink. It was only a foot away from the seat. Once the bunk was down, she realized, she'd have to kneel on the mattress in order to brush her teeth.

She pointed to a door. "Is that the bathroom?"

"Oh, no, that leads to another cabin. These are really wonderful cars. Each cabin can sleep two, so if a family is traveling together, the door between the two can be opened, and the kids can run back and forth."

They would have to be very tiny kids, Kaitlin decided, if they were going to run anywhere between these cabins. No bigger than dolls.

"The bathroom," he told her with pride, "is right here, behind the sink."

The bathroom...

There was a fiberglass toilet in a space that seemed to be two feet by two feet at the most. The shower head was in the wall. To use it, the toilet seat needed to be closed, and the water would just spray around the entire cubicle.

Well, she had wanted small and cozy. This was certainly that.

She smiled. "Thanks. I think I see where everything is, all right."

He grinned. "Great. If you need me, give a holler. I'm here to serve you."

She nodded and thanked him again. As he left, the train began to pull away from the station.

She heard thudding in the cabin connected to hers. Apparently her neighbor had arrived even later than she had.

She decided to settle in. She had hours and hours before they crossed the Georgia border.

She unpacked her toiletries, then took another look in the bathroom. It was so small that it made her shudder. She wondered what a larger person would do in such a space.

Well, it wasn't quite home, she thought a few minutes later, but everything was in its place and her suitcases were stowed away. She took off her shoes, curled up on the seat by the window and brought out a mystery novel by one of her favorite authors, a book she had been saving especially for this occasion.

She tried to read, but the first pages didn't seem to make sense. She read them over, then she realized that she was thinking about Brendan.

She leaned back and closed her eyes.

She would see Brendan again very soon, in two days. His secretary had called Janis to arrange a lunch meeting for them at the hall where they were having the party. They would go over the menu and check the seating arrangements. And they'd be together at the dinner, of course.

Then she wouldn't really need to see him again for a while. Barbara was having a standard shower, and Joe was having an all-male bachelor party. After this trip, weeks could go by before she had to see him again.

She didn't know whether she was relieved or anxious.

She set her book down, keeping her eyes closed. The motion of the train was gentle and soothing, and she drifted to sleep.

When she awoke she was amazed to discover that it was already dark outside. She glanced at her watch. It was almost six; she had slept for nearly eight hours. In a ridiculous position on the tiny seat. Her neck was cramped, and she was stiff and miserable. And hungry.

With a sigh she rose and stretched, then stumbled the fifteen inches to the tiny sink. She washed her face and combed out her hair, and decided that dinner seemed like a good idea. She had noticed that the dining car was forward when she boarded the train, so she walked that way, passing through another car of sleepers and one of seats.

There was a buffet line, and she joined it, then had to choose between chicken, fish and beef for the entrée. She decided on the breaded chicken and iced tea, then followed the attendant, who carried her tray along a line of tables.

She saw only the top of his head at first, yet even then, she felt little prickles along her skin. The attendant was still walking, but she was standing still in the aisle.

Then he raised his head. There was no mistaking him. Brendan was on the train. Sitting at a booth, sipping coffee and reading a newsmagazine. And now . . .

And now he was staring at her. He didn't smile, and he definitely looked surprised to see her.

Someone bumped into her from behind as the train jolted. She almost toppled over, but Brendan was instantly on his feet and down the aisle, catching her before she could fall.

It was another one of the waiters behind her, a sweet little man who began to apologize profusely. Kaitlin assured him that it was all right, all the while staring at Brendan.

"Let's sit down before this gets any worse, shall we?" he murmured, leading her to the booth where he had been sitting. Her food seemed to be long gone.

"What are you doing on this train?" she demanded, more sharply than she had intended. She winced inwardly. Why couldn't she be nice?

"Kaitlin, there are two trains a day out of Miami, one in the morning, one at night. This train was the only one I could take!"

"You should have taken an airplane!" she accused him.

"You could have flown," he reminded her.

"I hate to fly."

"You're terrified of flying."

"No, I'm not. I just hate to do it," she lied. "And I do fly."

"Yes, I've heard about the way you fly," he informed her, frowning. "Inebriated into insensibility. Barely conscious," he commented.

"That's why *you* should have flown!" she informed him.

He arched a brow. "I like trains, Kaitlin. I work on the train. I read on the train. I look at the countryside, and I even enjoy the seedy side of the landscape. And the last I heard, this is a free country, so why the hell can't I take a train if I so choose? Are you that afraid of me?"

"I'm not afraid of you!"

"Can't stay away from me, huh? Afraid you'll wind up sleeping with me because there won't be anywhere for you to run once you start things?"

"I am not going to sleep with you!" she exclaimed, far more loudly than she realized.

There was a crashing sound beside her. She looked over to realize that her attendant and the waiter who had bumped into her were both standing beside the table, one to bring a complimentary glass of wine, the other, who had found her at last, to deliver her dinner tray. Only he had dropped her tray, his face reddening, when he overheard their conversation.

She realized then that she must have spoken very loudly, because the diners around them were staring at her, too.

"Now look what you've done," Brendan told her.

She wanted to throttle him or, at the very least, dump the wine over his head. She gritted her teeth while the first waiter assured her that he'd be back with her dinner in just a minute. "I—I had lost you," he explained, picking up the remnants of the chicken from the aisle. She smiled sickly. Then the wine was set down, and both men hurried away.

Her fellow passengers, however, continued to stare for several seconds.

Brendan was smiling. "Want to leave?"

"With my tail between my legs? No, thanks," she assured him. There was still one pinched-faced lady staring at her. Kaitlin couldn't help herself. She gripped Brendan's hand passionately and leaned toward him. "All right, I *will* sleep with you again."

"Right here?"

"Have we got the space?"

"I guess not."

"We'll just have to wait."

The woman rose, wide-eyed. Brendan gave her a wink, and she huffed. Then he laughed, and Kaitlin found that she was smiling. "She's probably thinking that the trains really are filled with derelicts these days," he assured her.

She flushed. Her tray of food arrived, and she toyed with it idly, feeling his gaze. "It was all your fault," she told him.

"Mine?"

"For being on the train. I would never have stopped dead still if I hadn't seen you. And then the man wouldn't have rushed into me. And the other waiter wouldn't have lost me."

"I see. I'm guilty of existing."

She made a face and pushed her tray away. "You really should fly."

His lashes were heavy over his eyes as he leaned back, watching her. "So should you. It saves time." And then to her surprise, he rose. "I'll let you dine in peace, Ms. O'Herlihy." But he paused next to her and whispered softly, "Since you won't sleep with me here and now. Too bad. You had me all excited."

She spun around, but he was already starting down the aisle.

She stared at her food for a minute, decided that she wasn't hungry after all, then stood and left the waiter a tip. She started down the hallway, passed through the other cars to hers, where she stared at the letters on the cabin doors. The attendant had been in to pull down the bunks, and the drapes were pulled over the windows in the doors.

She came to cabin AA and opened it. The door slammed into something, and she shoved at it, certain that her luggage must have gotten in the way.

"Hey!" came an aggrieved voice. The door swung open, and she almost fell in.

Brendan was there. He was shirtless, taking up all the space between the lowered bunk and the sink. He glowered at her. "What are you doing?"

"This—this is my cabin."

"Sorry, it's mine."

She pointed to the letter on the door. "Brendan, I know it's my cabin."

"No, Kaitlin, it's mine." A woman was coming down the narrow hall. Kaitlin had to get out of her way, so she moved into the cabin, almost on top of him. He backed away from the door to give her room. Then he sighed with exasperation and drew her all the way in. He flicked a bolt on the door connecting his cabin to the one next door, opened it and thrust her through. She saw her belongings.

"You're cabin A—not AA," he told her, then turned, returning to the sink.

He hadn't closed the door. She followed him the three steps in. "Well, I'm sorry. Very sorry."

His head clunked into the medicine cabinet as he started to raise his face from the water. He hadn't quite been able to get his body bent into the space to begin with. He looked so angry that she thought he was going to start to growl.

He slammed his hands on the sink. "Sorry. How nice. You know, Kaitlin, I've never heard you say you were sorry about anything before."

"I haven't had anything to be sorry about!" she flared, swinging around and slamming the door between them. She took the two steps to her own sink, determined to brush her teeth, wash her face and curl up with her book again. She could—and would—forget that he was there next to her.

But the connecting door slammed open again, and he was standing there, legs spread, bare chested, his hair damp, his eyes glittering. "Because everything was always my fault, right, Kaitlin?"

She turned. He was walking toward her, and she was trapped in the tiny space between the bunk and the sink.

"Yes," she said simply.

"I never filed papers against you!" he rasped out furiously.

She gasped, then fell silent for a moment. He had never protested, never tried to contact her, never said a word.

Not until this moment had she realized that their divorce had meant anything to him at all.

"You—you left me!" she whispered.

"I joined the Navy," he said more quietly. "Because I thought you wanted more out of life than I could give you."

"I did want more. But I wanted it from you," she said.

He was standing at least a foot away. She could see the rise and fall of his chest, the damp sprinkles of water upon it, the rippling of the muscles there. He lifted his hands. "All that we had," he murmured. "All that we had, and we could never talk."

Tears were rising behind her eyelids, dampening her lashes. She gritted her teeth to keep the tears from falling.

He turned, starting to go to his own cabin. "Well, it's too late for this now, isn't it?" he murmured softly. "Good night, Kaitlin."

He disappeared through the door and closed it behind him. She stared at it for a moment, her hands on her hips. Then she strode toward it and flung it open. He had just stripped off his jeans and was standing by the bunk in his briefs. She paused for a moment, staring at him, then she inhaled sharply and stared into his eyes.

"You didn't even come home when I lost the baby!" she flared.

"I didn't know!" he snapped.

"You had to know. I wrote to you—"

"And I was already on a ship. Kaitlin, it was the Navy, not a joyride!" He was walking toward her. She had to retreat. She needed time to assimilate the things they were saying. She spun, but he caught her arm and turned her back. He ran his free hand through his hair. "Kaitlin, damn it, you know I would have come if I had known!"

She tried desperately to free herself. He released her, and she crashed into the door to the bath and fell on the commode, bringing him with her. Then the door slammed shut on them both. They might have been a pair of sardines caught in a too-small can.

Brendan swore, finding it impossible even to turn around. Kaitlin, caught beneath him, tried to catch hold of something and rise.

Her fingers closed over the rubber shower arm, and suddenly water was spraying all over them.

"Damnation, Kaitlin—" He managed to shut off the water, then find the catch on the door. When he swung it open, he turned for her, pulling her over the step, soaked and sodden, in his arms.

They both started to laugh. Her skirt was plastered against her body, and her hair was slicked against her head. She was touching him, and she could feel the dampness of his briefs—the heat beneath them.

Then their laughter faded. Suddenly they were staring at one another. Emotions simmered, seeming to rise like steam between them.

Kaitlin started to tremble and tried to pull away, but Brendan's hands were tight on her arms, and he held her flush against him. She went still as, slowly, slowly, his head descended toward hers. His lips, hot and wet, moved over hers, and his tongue invaded her mouth, all of him warm and wet and assertive. The fingers of his right hand tangled into her damp hair as his left hand pressed into the small of her back, bringing her more tightly against him. As he freely tasted her mouth, the resistance within her faded. He stroked both hands down the length of her back, cupped her buttocks and brought her up high against the rising steel of his desire.

He kissed her until she knew that she had no strength within her, until she was weak from the wonder and intimacy of his body against hers. Her clothes and his briefs seemed to offer no real barrier between them. And he was still kissing her. Finding her lips, playing his tongue over her earlobe, her throat, her cheeks, her lips. Licking, taunting, probing the deep recesses of her mouth.

Then he pulled away, holding her cheeks, studying her eyes. She knew that her lips were wet and swollen, that her expression was dazed, and he smiled slowly, and with pain.

"I can't seduce you," he whispered.

"No," she agreed.

"And you're not going to sleep with me on the train."

"That's what I said I'd do," she murmured.

"But then again, you were going to have sex with me right on the dining room table."

"Between the rolls and the wine," she agreed, her whisper swallowed up by his soft kiss. Then the teasing quality left his voice, and he told her, "I can't just date you, Kaitlin. I thought that was what we needed, at first. But just like I can't change the pain of the past, I can't change the intimacy of it. I can't pretend that you were never mine, or that I don't want you now. I don't expect you to swear away your life to me. I don't want promises, or a commitment. But I do need honesty."

She didn't quite understand what he was saying to her. It could have been so easy. He had just kissed her, and their passion had risen and soared. They could have followed through to the natural conclusion without awkwardness, without a word being exchanged. And she knew that he still wanted her, desperately. She could feel the pulse and the heat of his wanting. Feel it make her want him in return...

She shook her head slightly and dampened her lips. "What do you want from me, Brendan? I can't make the years disappear, either. You say you don't want promises, but what promises could we give one another, anyway? I can't erase the pain either. And I..."

"And you what?" he demanded, his green gaze fierce as he stared at her.

"I can't just date you, either, I suppose. I don't know. I don't..." She shook her head. "What do you want?" she whispered.

And he told her. He leaned down, his lips against her ear, his whisper soft and yet searing. And his thumb trailed down her spine, and he drew her close once again.

"I want you to want me," he told her. "No repercussions, no running away in the morning. I just want you to want me."

She met his eyes again and smiled very slowly. She reached up, wrapping her arms around him, pulling his lips to hers. And she kissed him with an ardor to match his, tasting his lips with her tongue, fusing them sweetly together in an ardent dance of desire. Then she spoke against his lips, her lashes heavy against her eyes. "I wanted you at my house that night. When you left."

"The night when you didn't even know that we hadn't made love when it was all over?" he whispered, and she flushed. He shook his head. "I promised you that you'd remember," he said softly. "Tell me you want me now."

His hands were on her blouse, undoing the small buttons. He didn't fumble, his fingers moving even as his eyes met hers.

She inhaled sharply as his knuckles grazed over the flesh of her breast.

"I want you now," she told him.

He stripped away her shirt and let it fall to the floor. He kissed her shoulder blades, lifting her lacy bra straps and pulling them sensually down her arms, then releasing the snaps in back. At last he lowered his head, taking her breast into his mouth, laving the nipple with his tongue, then suckling hard on the peak so that she arched against him in a sudden swift rush of sensation so sharp that she cried out softly. Suddenly he was kneeling before her, finding the zipper to her skirt, pulling it down slowly. She stepped from her clothes, and he teased the flesh at her waist, then swept away her pantyhose and bikinis in a quick motion before burying his face against the softness of her belly.

He caught her buttocks and brought her hard against him as he kissed her abdomen and upper thighs. She closed her eyes, throwing her head back in response. And she trembled, wondering what he would do next, the anticipation exciting her nearly as desperately as the touch that followed.

For when he touched her so intimately, the shock tore through her system, the sweetness pervaded her, and she could not think. She could barely stand as she felt the delicious rush drenching her inside with hot, honeyed wonder. Then the world seemed to burst into brilliance and rush into black, and she could not stand. She was falling as the nectar and the ecstasy spilled from her.

She was in his arms as she fell, and he was catching her so that she landed on the lower bunk. He kissed her, and her fingers raked over his back, then slipped beneath the waistband of his briefs. Lovingly, slowly, she peeled them down, stroking the flesh of his hips, her fingers moving to the soft down at his navel, then closing around the hard, pulsing life of him. He groaned, shuddering, and wedged his way between her thighs, then caught her hands and curled her fingers within his own, and plunged deep within her.

She cried out softly, loving the feel of him within her. Then he began to move, and she felt as if the earth itself was shifting beneath her. He stroked the flesh within her, touched, caressed and teased, then plunged deeply again, cradling her against him, savoring the sensation of being locked so tightly together. Slowly, then swiftly, he moved, and she rocked with him, sweetly aware that she was straining against him, wanting more of him, closing around him. She could feel the sheen of perspiration that covered her body and his, and the ever spiraling hunger that drove them both. Then release burst upon her, and she trembled and shook with the strength of her response. She felt the force of his body shuddering against hers again and again, felt the heated rush of his seed filling her.

And still he lay taut against her, holding her close. Then he groaned softly against her throat, kissed her, nipped her flesh and kissed it again. And in the growing shadows he lifted his head, and she saw that he was smiling. Only then did she realize that they were really only half on the bunk, and that he was twisted in a truly unreasonable position. She pulled him over her, stretching out against the wall of the cabin. They barely fit onto the bunk together.

"You know, Ms. O'Herlihy," he whispered softly against her cheek, his fingers tenderly, idly stroking her flesh from her collarbone to her breast, "there have been numerous times—numerous times!—when we have been alone near sumptuous, comfortable beds. Beds with space, with softness, with support, with clean, fresh sheets and endless pillows. And you pick a two-by-four train car."

"What?" she demanded, struggling to sit up.

"I may never walk again," he told her solemnly.

"Oh!"

He laughed, pulling her close again. And his whisper filled her ear sweetly. "It was worth it. Whatever the sacrifice, it was worth it."

"Sacrifice!"

"My spine is a pretzel."

"Well, I'll just go to my own cabin, then!" she told him.

He shook his head. "Not on your life, Kaitlin O'Herlihy," he told her, carefully balancing his weight, his green gaze somehow sharp and tender and wicked all at once. "This is an odyssey, a challenge…an adventure." He lowered himself against her slowly, still smiling.

The train whistled shrilly in the darkness, but neither of them noticed as he began to kiss and arouse her again, feeling the rebirth of a hot and flickering fire within him.

She shimmied down his body, giving in to every decadent and wanton desire that had ever filled her fantasies, touching him, caressing him, tormenting his hips and chest with tiny flicks of her tongue, rubbing her body against his. The space at their disposal was quite limited, but this *was* an adventure....

She breathed in the masculine scent that had haunted her dreams for years. She tasted the salty remnants of their love against his flesh. She teased and taunted with her hair and lips, kissing and arousing him everywhere until at last she closed her fingers around his renewed desire. Unbearably aroused herself, she kissed, she caressed.

Until he swore and proved that he could fit fully atop her, despite the limitations of the bunk.

The whistle shrilled again, or it could have been her cry of desire, of ecstasy fulfilled.

The night went on and on, as she lay against him, his arms around her, and he whispered with a trace of amusement and a satisfied shudder, "Beyond a doubt, Kaitlin, me love...this is the way to see America!"

Chapter 9

As it happened, it was one of the best train rides Kaitlin had ever taken. In more ways than one.

She was glad she had slept all day, because she didn't sleep a wink during the night. And since they would have to change trains very early in New York, Brendan suggested with a sigh that they should rise at about five-thirty to shower and dress.

Then, listening to Brendan swear vociferously as he tried to fit in the shower and bathe at the same time, she laughed as she was sure she hadn't laughed in years. He heard her and came bolting out, soaked and sudsy and insisting she come in and help him. She swore that they wouldn't fit, but somehow they managed. And then he began to tickle her, until she was laughing and gasping at the same time, and they wound up making love one last time and having to shower all over again.

She slipped into her own cabin in time for the attendant to deliver her coffee and croissants, then she breakfasted while she applied her makeup. She had barely finished when the attendant came by again, warning her that they were about to reach New York.

Brendan came to get her luggage down, and they detrained together. The layover in New York was a little more than an hour, plenty of time to have a second cup of coffee and pick up a newspaper.

Kaitlin was surprised at just how warm and wonderful it felt to hurry for the next train together, to have him take her bags, hold her hand, be with her. She hadn't realized just how alone she had been.

This time they were on a commuter train, sitting in regular seats, with dozens of people around them. They didn't talk at all. He was reading a magazine, and she took out her mystery. Somehow, with Brendan beside her, she found herself absolutely delighted by the book, and she read on, turning the pages faster and faster until she realized that they had arrived in Boston.

They detrained again and walked to the street. And there a bit of the bubble burst, because they had to separate, having ordered rental cars from different companies.

"Do you really need a car?" Brendan asked her.

She nodded. "I'll be running around with Donna and

you'll be running around with Bill. And I'm not staying with my parents, either. I decided on a motel in
Auburn because I really didn't know what hours I
would be keeping.''

"I'm not staying with my parents, either."

"I suppose you're staying at your own place?"

He shook his head. "I told you—it's too far out."
Then he smiled wickedly. "But, since the choices in
Auburn are limited, I'm willing to bet we're staying at
the same motel."

She smiled slowly. "I wonder if maybe I shouldn't
go home after all."

"Oh?"

"My father could protect me."

He scowled. "Kaitlin, I didn't—"

"You didn't," she interrupted, then added quickly,
"not from you. From myself."

"Tell you what. I'll cancel my car, we'll take yours
into Worcester, and I'll get myself a car there."

She lowered her eyes quickly. Her heart was beating furiously, and she was ridiculously pleased because they were going to be spending a little more time
together. They were going to be staying at the same
motel. But they would be running around with Donna and Bill, and their time together would be limited.

He was already on the street, hailing a cab. He must
have had the knack, because one came along instantly. They had the driver take them to the rental car
company by the airport. Kaitlin stepped forward to
pick up her car, and Brendan waited for her. When she

had finished the paperwork, she met him with the keys in her hand. "Want to drive?"

"Sure." He took the keys from her, and she smiled.

"I hate the Boston traffic. I'm not here enough. I always make a wrong turn and end up going in circles."

"Well, I've got a confession to make," he told her. "I still go in circles now and then, too."

But he didn't make any mistakes. He knew the expressway and the way to the turnpike, and from there it was simple.

He drove to Worcester, to another rental agency, parked and got out. Then he leaned over and kissed her lightly on the lips. "I'll see you later?"

She nodded. He retrieved his luggage, then stepped back and waved. She twisted the key and drove away.

By six o'clock that night she had checked into the motel, driven out to a neighboring town to see her parents and come back to Auburn to meet Donna for dinner. They hugged fiercely, not just relatives but friends all their lives. Donna, with her dark auburn hair and light blue eyes, looked enough like Kaitlin to be her sister. They had shared everything throughout the years, their opinions on boys, on clothing and music, then, when they had matured, their ideas on morality and ethics. Kaitlin was happy for Donna, but what should have been an easy occasion was suddenly very hard for her.

Things had changed last night. Unbelievably. She didn't know what to think or feel, and she wanted to spill out the whole story to her cousin and ask for advice. She wanted to cry for help, but she was also desperate to keep her own counsel. She was more afraid than ever. Get out of my heart and out of my mind! she silently warned an absent Brendan as she listened to Donna's enthusiasm, looked at the picture of the dress she had ordered and praised the bridesmaids' dresses Donna liked.

They talked about the wedding, and Donna talked about Bill, and Kaitlin kept the subject away from herself for hours. They ate dinner, then went to the bridal shop at the mall, where Kaitlin was fitted for her gown. Then they took a ride to the reception hall and went by the church to listen to the organist and choose the music.

Finally they stopped for a drink at a club near Kaitlin's motel, and Donna asked her how the train ride had been.

"The train ride?" Kaitlin murmured, stalling.

"Sure, how was it? Boring?"

Boring. Kaitlin lowered her eyes and ran her fingers over the table. "Uh, no, it wasn't boring."

"Long?"

"It, uh, it didn't seem that long, either." She kept her lashes lowered. Laughter was welling up inside her. She wanted to tell Donna about the episode in the shower. Donna would laugh, too, just like when they were young.

But she couldn't say anything, no matter how close they were. The future was more frightening to her than it had ever been before.

Finally she raised her eyes and looked at Donna. "Brendan was on the same train."

"Oh! That's right, Bill told me he likes to take the train, that he needs the time."

"Yes, something like that."

"Well?" Donna's eyes were wide, and there was a whisper of excitement in her voice. "Well?"

"Well, what?" Kaitlin asked smoothly.

"Are you two getting along? Are the sparks flying?"

"We're both in your wedding party. And we want the wedding to be great. We're working well enough together."

"And that's all?" Donna asked.

"That's all," Kaitlin lied sweetly.

"But he made the train ride go more quickly, huh? You two talked. He was entertaining?"

"Oh, uh, very entertaining."

She realized Donna was grinning and looking past her. She whirled around to see that Bill and Brendan had come into the club and were standing behind her. Her cheeks reddened. Brendan was tossing his jacket over the chair beside her and taking a seat, his green eyes flashing with amusement.

"Kaitlin was darned entertaining, too, Donna," he told her. He said it with a very straight face.

Kaitlin cast him a quick glare, then rose to kiss and hug Bill. Then she sat, and the men ordered drinks.

The conversation flowed smoothly. At least, Kaitlin thought it did. She wasn't really a part of it; she just listened. And she felt Brendan so close beside her, and a chill streaked up and down her spine.

It might have been years ago. They'd all known each other so long. They'd taken day trips together as kids, long rides out to the cape, excursions into New Hampshire and Maine. Nights in New York City. It might have been forever ago.

But it wasn't. She didn't really know Brendan anymore. She had to keep telling herself that. He didn't want to date, but despite what had happened on the train, she was afraid to rush. They'd hurt one another too badly in the past.

Suddenly she rose, kissed them all—even Brendan—and excused herself, saying that she was exhausted. She promised Brendan she would meet him at noon at the restaurant where they'd be having the party, and she told Donna and Bill she'd see them the next night. Then she left.

At the door, she felt Brendan's gaze and turned. He was staring after her intently, but she couldn't begin to read his expression, or his mind.

She met him at noon, as promised. He was precise and cool as they went over the menu, checked on the entertainment and listened to the war stories the maître d' had to tell them. But when they were seated alone with sandwiches for lunch, he wasted no time.

"What was going on last night?" he asked her tensely.

"Nothing."

He almost smiled. "It was definitely nothing," he agreed. "Why did you walk away?"

"I was tired."

"It was more than that."

"All right," she said softly. "You want to know what happened last night? I was afraid."

"Of me?"

She leaned forward, plunging in. "Yes, of you. Brendan, we were divorced almost eight years ago. We were married for less than two. And when I went to the Keys to see you that time, one night destroyed my equilibrium for another year. I don't want to fall for you again. We didn't just hurt each other before—it was torture."

He leaned back, staring at her. "So what do you want to do?" he asked softly.

"I—I don't know."

"Run away from it?"

She was silent, afraid that he would stand up and walk away, that they would never have a chance to really talk again.

What she wanted, she realized, was a declaration of undying love and devotion, a promise that they would make it. She wanted him to say that he had loved her forever, that there had never been anyone else.

But he couldn't tell her that, and she knew it. There was too much time, and too much distance, between them.

"I don't know what I want," she said very softly.

He rose, and she thought he was going to storm away. But he didn't. He touched her cheek lightly. "I *do* know what I want," he said quietly.

And then he walked away.

When she followed moments later, he was nowhere to be seen.

At the motel she sat by her phone, staring at it, thinking she should call him and suggest that they drive to the party together—they were coming from the same place. But she couldn't quite manage to dial. No, she couldn't even manage to pick up the receiver. Brendan should have called her.

But he wasn't going to. Not after the way they had left things at the restaurant.

She showered and dressed with plenty of time to spare. Then she sat by the telephone again. She had just about convinced herself to pick up the receiver when there was a knock at her door. She hurried over and threw it open.

Brendan was there. "I wondered if you were ready," he said. She nodded, not trusting herself to speak. He was striking in his dove-gray suit, white shirt and maroon vest. His hair was clean and damp, a shining ebony. He wore clothes well, she decided.

And when he didn't wear clothes...

Her mind was slipping. "I'm ready," she said, and she was breathless. "But it's too early to head out—"

"Let's take a ride," he told her.

She didn't know where they were going, but she nodded. He picked up her shawl and drew it around her shoulders, then caught her hand and walked her along the hall.

They still hadn't spoken when he seated her in his car, and she asked him softly, "Where are we going?"

His lips curved slowly into a smile as he stared ahead at the road. "I don't know," he admitted, and she smiled, too.

The car might have been a horse, allowed to take its own lead. They just started driving, and suddenly they were in the heart of Worcester, driving by the old neighborhood. They went by the triple decker where the O'Herlihys had first lived, then down to Burncoat Street, where her father had built their first house. They went by the high school and the pool and the park, and then they decided to see if the best little family-run Italian restaurant in town was still in business. It was.

"Too bad we're out of time," Brendan said morosely.

She laughed. "Brendan, we're throwing a dinner party. An expensive dinner party, at that. And you want to stop for pasta first?"

He nodded. "Yeah, but we haven't got the time."

He started driving again, and Kaitlin felt a faint and curious prickling along her spine. They were passing the cemetery where members of both their families had been buried. Including Sean.

"You think the gates might still be open?" she asked.

He glanced at her sharply. Dusk was falling. He glanced at the car clock. "There're about ten minutes left. Why?"

"Let's go in."

"Kaitlin—"

"Please, Brendan, I want to."

He shrugged, then swung the car around the corner and through the gates. He drove as far as he could, then pulled the car up to the side of the road.

The cemetery was very quiet. There didn't seem to be another soul there. To the left, the old slate tombstones that gave credence to the cemetery's age rose against the twilight. Here, in the newer section, there was a multitude of beautiful twentieth-century stones. Praying angels, saints, obelisks, all kinds of memorials to loved ones who had passed from the world.

Kaitlin didn't head for the bowing angel above the graves of her father's parents and grandparents. She walked straight to the large statue of a beautiful Saint Theresa standing guard over the earthly remains of Sean O'Herlihy.

In the dusk, Saint Theresa seemed almost to live and breathe. And there was a gentle, curious smile on her lips that reminded Kaitlin of Sean.

Brendan was standing behind her, and he didn't come any closer.

There were flowers on the grave.

"You've been here already," she said.

"I've been here," he told her. "But I didn't bring the flowers. Someone in the family always brings flowers at this time every year."

Kaitlin nodded, staring at the grave. Suddenly she wanted to cry as badly as she had all those years ago. What would have happened if Sean had lived? Would she and Brendan be celebrating more than a decade of marriage? Would there have been other children to replace the one they had lost? It was a mystery, buried deep within the earth with Sean O'Herlihy.

"We should go," Brendan said, and she nodded. He led her from the grave and helped her into the car. And when they had moved into the traffic he asked her, "Why did you want to stop?"

"I don't know."

"Kaitlin, he's been dead for twelve years."

She glanced at him sharply. "Has he ever really died for you, Brendan?"

He frowned, catching her eyes in the rear view mirror. "I'll never forget him, if that's what you're saying. He was my best friend. Any time you lose someone, a certain emptiness remains."

She didn't answer him, only looked out the window. Then she murmured softly, "He left us because he had no choice. But the emptiness was worse when you left me, too, because you didn't have to go."

He suddenly pulled the car onto the sidewalk.

"What are you talking about?" he demanded.

"Brendan, you're on the damn sidewalk!"

"I don't care! Answer me!"

"I was still there, Brendan. And you were still there. But you left me. You were gone. Sean didn't leave on purpose. You did. You had a choice."

"I didn't leave."

"You weren't there."

He leaned back against the seat and swore. "What the hell do you want from me, Kaitlin? I've said I was wrong. I've tried to explain. I know you understood. You were wonderful, you were quiet and supportive, and you just waited. And I hurt you. I'm sorry." He swung around to face her. "Maybe I was even wrong later, when I caught you with another guy—"

"It was nothing!" she choked out furiously.

"I just said I was wrong!" he told her harshly. "But once we were married, I wasn't the one to end it all with the clean stroke of a knife! What the hell was it? You didn't get the wedding you wanted, so you decided you had to try again? I'm surprised you didn't bargain for an annulment from the first. Then you could have had everything you wanted."

Eyes burning, she turned toward him, telling him exactly what she thought he was, her hand suddenly flying. She didn't slap his cheek only because he caught her wrist. And then she was in his arms again, his kiss searing her lips with a passion and fury and trembling vehemence more volatile than anything that had passed between them before. His lips and tongue tasted of his fury, his violence, of despair and of longing. The kiss spoke of time and of tears, and it seemed to shatter her heart.

He released her slowly, staring into her eyes. She felt a dampness on her cheeks, and she knew she was crying.

"Oh, Kaitlin," he whispered.

He kissed her very lightly then, and drew out his handkerchief, dabbing at her mouth. "I cut your lip," he said with regret. "I'm sorry, Kaitlin. Really."

She shook her head, taking the handkerchief as he revved the motor and eased the car into traffic. Darkness surrounded them, and the streetlights played across his features. Kaitlin wiped her cheeks and dabbed at her lips, and her heart suddenly ached as she watched him. She wondered if she had ever felt closer to him than she did at that moment, and she wondered how that could be.

Swallowing her pride and the pain that had built up over the years, she moved closer, laying her hand gently on his thigh. "I didn't really want a divorce, Brendan," she said in rush. "It was just that when I lost the baby, I was so hurt and so alone, and I wanted you so badly. And you didn't come—"

"I couldn't come! I didn't even know at first!"

"I know that now," she said. "But then, even when you were with me, you were still living in your own world. Brendan, I wanted you to protest. I wanted you to fight me. I wanted you to mourn Sean and our baby. I just wanted you to realize that we were both still alive!"

He didn't say anything for a long moment. Then he held the steering wheel with his left hand, and his right hand curved over hers.

Then they were at the restaurant, and he was swinging into the parking lot. He found a spot for the car and turned off the engine, then turned to her. He took the handkerchief from her and dabbed at her lip. "Damn, it looks like I gave you a good one to the jaw."

She laughed. "It can't be that bad. Oh, well, we'll chalk it all up to that Irish temper of yours."

"My Irish temper!"

She smiled, and so did he, but then his smile faded. "I gave you the divorce because I thought that it was what you wanted," he said. "How could I protest when everything had gone so badly?"

She shook her head, afraid she would start crying all over again.

"All those years," he murmured. "Kaitlin, I—"

She never knew what he had intended to say, because there was a tap at his window. They both started and turned their heads. Kaitlin's cousin Patrick was standing there, smiling. "Hey, you guys coming in or what?"

He walked around to open Kaitlin's door. "Patrick!" she murmured with forced enthusiasm. Patrick was great—she loved him. But she wondered why he'd had to show up at that exact moment. Still, she got out and gave him a big hug.

Brendan was out of the car, too, and beside them both, greeting Patrick. Then the three of them walked into the restaurant together.

It was a wonderful party. More than wonderful. Donna and Bill looked so happy together. Brendan gave the groom a great speech, and Donna received all sorts of beautiful things. Both families were there; the meal was delicious, and the band Brendan had hired played a range of songs that appealed to every age group.

They didn't leave until nearly 2:00 a.m. Donna and Bill stayed to the last, thanking them both profusely.

"It wasn't anything," Brendan told Donna.

"Yes, it was," Donna insisted. "It was wonderful. I just wish you two didn't have to lay out quite so much—"

"Honestly, it was nothing. Kaitlin has a new business," Brendan told her solemnly.

"Brendan's in on it, too," Kaitlin said sweetly. She explained about the commercial, then wished she hadn't. Now everyone in the world was going to be looking for it. She'd never hear the end of it from her relatives.

Donna went on and on, but finally she and Bill left, and Kaitlin and Brendan walked to his rental car. She leaned her head back as soon as she touched the seat. She was exhausted, drained.

He drove to the motel in silence, then escorted her up to her room. When she stopped by the door, he paused, then kissed her lips gently. She waited, tired, but growing flushed with excitement. He was going to stay, she thought. He would come in with her, and they would make love.

But he only told her good night very softly, then turned and walked away.

Kaitlin carefully disrobed and hung up her dress, then slipped into a soft flannel gown. Then she lay down and tried to sleep, but suddenly she felt the dampness on her cheeks, silent tears again, tears for all they had shared, all they had lost.

The love had never died. They had just thrown it away.

Perhaps everything was out in the open between them now. But could anything they said make it right now? Or had too much time passed, too many years? Could they ever rectify the past?

She lay awake for a long time, but exhaustion finally claimed her.

She was awakened very early by a pounding on her door. She hadn't even blinked enough to be coherent, but she bounded out of bed and threw open the door.

It was Brendan. An irritated Brendan. "Look at you, Kaitlin. Barely dressed, just throwing that door wide open. Hell, I could have been anyone. A burglar, a rapist!"

She stared at him blankly. "It's nice to see you, too, Brendan."

"Kaitlin, I'd just rather you didn't get yourself killed."

She nodded. "Sure." She shook her head. "Excuse me for a moment, will you?"

"Briefly," he warned her.

She shut herself into the bathroom and doused her head in cold water, then scrubbed her teeth. She felt lucid again.

When she walked out of the bathroom, she didn't see him at first, and she thought he had left.

Then he called her name softly. "Kaitlin."

She whirled and stared at him, stunned for a moment; then her lips slowly curved into a smile.

He was stretched out on her bed, stark naked. It could have been a calendar pose if it hadn't looked so natural. He was glorious and tempting beyond all measure, leaning on one elbow, his head resting on his hand, watching her. One ebony lock fell with a slightly rakish air over his forehead, and his green eyes were gleaming, the gold specks seeming to catch the morning sun. He was all bronze muscle, the thick thatch of dark hair on his chest immensely inviting. And below that . . . his intent was certainly visible.

"Come here," he said, patting the bed.

"What the hell are you doing?" she whispered.

"You'll have a good time, I promise," he told her with absolute confidence.

She still hadn't moved, so he did. He rose and walked over to her, and deftly began to undo the tiny buttons on her flannel gown. She still didn't make a move, but she allowed him to strip her, paradoxically feeling both lethargy and excitement sweep through her as the gown fell to the floor. He moved behind her, and she felt his naked body brushing her back and buttocks. His hands curled around her breasts, and his lips brushed heat and fire against her ear as his tongue dampened her flesh in small circles. He swept her hair aside, and his kiss moved down the length of her spine. She turned in his arms, choking as the sensations of sweet fire claimed her. His tongue dipped into her navel and flicked along her belly. Unable to stand any longer, she knelt before him and caught his lips in a fierce and hungry kiss.

He meant to sweep her into his arms, to carry her over to the endless soft expanse of the bed. To make love to her there. But her lips were on his, her fingers moving over his back, stroking, while their tongues met and mated in an age-old rhythm. And she was there, beneath his hands. So he touched her. He teased her legs apart and feathered his fingers over the juncture of her thighs, then teased the bud of her desire and probed deeply into the heart of her sexuality. Her soft cries aroused him to a frenzy, and it seemed that her hands were beautifully, miraculously everywhere. On his shoulders, taunting his buttocks, curling around the very life and strength and force of him. Touching him, stroking him, until he thought he would die if he didn't take her soon.

He laid her on the thick carpet and wedged her legs apart, convinced—in his heart, in his mind, in his hunger—that she could never forget this morning. And then he had her with the force of his kiss and his tongue, parting her fiercely, tasting her endlessly. Ignoring her cries and her pleas, and taking an ever-increasing pleasure in the wild undulations of her body as he forced a searing burst of ecstasy upon her, tasting the response of her body to his hunger and demand.

He did not let her drift down, but wrapped her in his embrace and cried out hoarsely, plunging the need of his body into the promise of hers, shaking as she gloved him with warmth and fire and liquid heat. Tender, violent, he rode out his desire. Felt her move, her legs locking around his back, and breathed out words of passion, burying his face against her throat, then his lips against her breast. He felt her stiffen, heard her cry, and knew the sweet liquid flooding around him once again. And he sank into her, shuddering, climaxing, and praying that he could fill her with the love that had been lost to them both for so long.

He closed his eyes and held her.

Then, slowly, they both became aware of the hum of the air conditioner and movement in the hall outside the door. The world was awakening.

He turned to look at her. At the blue beauty of her eyes, at the sheen of perspiration covering her, the damp strawberry-blond locks tangling over her breasts and cheeks. He moved her hair, smiling. "What is it that you have against beds, Kaitlin?"

"Me!" she protested.

He stared at her, loving her, and kissed her lips again, very slowly. "I'd want you anywhere," he told her. "Anywhere at all."

Then, to Kaitlin's amazement, he rose and stretched a hand to her, still grinning. "Although it would be nice to try a bed next time." His smile eased, and his eyes searched hers. "If there is a next time," he said softly.

He turned and walked into her shower. Stunned, she listened as the water started. She walked to the bathroom door.

"What do you think you're doing, Brendan?" she asked, and tried the door. It was locked.

He was quick, though, emerging moments later, toweling himself strenuously. He paused to lightly kiss her lips, then dressed. "I'm going home, Kaitlin. I fly out in about two hours. I've got to get back to Boston."

She felt her temper soaring. "Nice of you to stop by," she told him.

He reached for the coverlet, wrapping it around her shoulders. She tried to wrench away from him, but she couldn't. He laughed easily, still holding her.

"Brendan—"

His finger fell across her lips. "I told you yesterday, Kaitlin. I know what I want. You don't. So think about it. Take your time. Neither of us can undo all the things we did before. We've thrown away years of our lives. Let's not do it again."

"Brendan, I—"

"I don't want you to say anything. Think about it. I'm going to go home and go to work. I'll see you at Donna and Bill's wedding. And when I see you again, I want an answer!"

Then he was gone, and she was left to stare after him, dressed only in the coverlet.

"An answer to what, Brendan?" she shouted.

She sank down on the bed, and she didn't know whether to laugh or cry.

"An answer to what, Brendan?" she repeated softly. "An answer to what?"

Chapter 10

Nearly four weeks later, Kaitlin was again in Massachusetts.

She'd gone home, gone to work, had a very traditional all-girl shower for her cousin Barbara. And she and Barbara had ordered flowers, checked on the menu and listened to bands. They'd run around looking for favors for the reception table, and they'd made a very elegant little box where gifts of money could be safely left.

They'd survived a few rough spots, like the reception hall sending out a warning that it might file for bankruptcy before Barbara's wedding. Barbara had called, hysterical, and she and Kaitlin had hurried to the hall, only to be assured that things had already changed, that new money had been invested in the business, and everything would be perfect.

Kaitlin didn't see Brendan. Brendan told her that he and Bill and some others were going to be taking off for a special one-night cruise to Freeport and back. Later she heard that they had gone, but that the hotel had been overbooked, and they'd had to wait until nearly 2:00 a.m. to get rooms, and one room had been filled with bedbugs.

She hoped it had been Brendan's room. He deserved bedbugs.

But Joe laughed when she asked him about it, and told her that despite their problems, they'd all had the time of their lives.

And still she didn't hear from Brendan.

Before she knew it, it was time to leave for Donna's wedding.

There was plenty to do when she arrived in Auburn. She and Donna covered what seemed like half of Massachusetts in a matter of days. They drove to one small town for the special ribbons Donna wanted on the flowers, then to another to deliver the ribbons. They picked up the elegant party favors that Donna and Patrick and his wife had painstakingly been making for weeks, then they brought them to the hall. They went for the last fitting on the gowns and agreed to pick them up at ten o'clock on the day of the wedding.

"We'll bring them all to my mother's house and get dressed there," Donna said. "Bill and the guys can dress at his house."

Finally the day of the rehearsal dinner arrived.

Tremors had set into Kaitlin with the sure knowledge that she would see Brendan that night. She had chosen her dress with care for that very reason. It was sheer black satin and covered her from neck to knee, but it fit her so closely that it was one of the sexiest things she had ever seen.

She wondered if Brendan was staying at the motel, but she doubted it. She wasn't staying there herself this time. With the wedding so close, she was rooming with Donna at her mother's house.

At six-thirty they left for the rehearsal. The church was already filled with family and friends.

And then Kaitlin saw Brendan. He was across the aisle, talking to one of Bill's ushers, when he caught sight of her.

His eyes moved up and down her so pointedly that she flushed and turned away. Her little cousin, Brandy, was about to start attacking the candles, so she chased quickly after her. Then her mother found her and whispered, "What's taking so long?"

Startled, Kaitlin told her, "I don't know."

Then Barbara came by, almost in tears. "We've lost an usher."

"What do you mean, you've lost an usher?"

"Terry Simmons isn't here. He's forgotten the wedding! He's left the country—I'm sure of it!"

"Barbara, don't cry, don't panic. He's just late. He'll be here," Kaitlin assured her.

But as it turned out, they didn't have to find another body. Brendan managed to track Terry down at his office. He had merely written down the wrong time for the rehearsal. The priest paced, Barbara wept and Brandy tried to eat the candles while they all waited.

When Terry appeared he apologized profusely to Donna, and she kissed him and hugged him and told him she didn't give a damn, as long as he was finally there.

Kaitlin caught Brendan's eye and saw that he was smiling with amusement. She smiled, and the rehearsal was on.

Bill's mother had arranged for the dinner at a country club. Kaitlin and Brendan would be sitting with Donna and Bill, as well as another couple from the bridal party.

Brendan looked striking that night. No matter how elegant his clothes, the rugged planes of his face gave him an aura of masculinity that was sharp and appealing.

He didn't touch her after the rehearsal. He had led her along the aisle, and they had stood together beside Donna and Bill. But once they left the church, he didn't touch her.

Except with his eyes. And the look in them was decadent.

Dinner was delicious. The conversation flowed smoothly, and the champagne was great. Kaitlin knew she was drinking too much champagne again, but she couldn't help it. She was flushed, her palms damp. She wanted to be alone with Brendan. She wanted to watch him.

She wanted him to touch her. . . .

And she still wasn't the least bit sure what question she was supposed to be answering.

Apparently she wasn't going to find out, either. When dinner was over, he helped her out of her chair. "Watch the champagne tomorrow night," he warned her. "I'll see you then."

Early the next morning she discovered that she wasn't going to have to wait until the wedding to see him after all.

Donna had asked him to follow them to pick up the dresses because the gowns were bulky, and they needed the extra space in his car to carry them. When they arrived at the bridal shop, Donna went to the counter to speak with her consultant.

Brendan came over to Kaitlin. "Have you been thinking?" he asked tensely.

"You son of a bitch!" she hissed softly. "I've been doing nothing but thinking, and I don't even know what the hell it is I'm supposed to be thinking about!"

Before he could reply, Donna let out a cry of distress.

They stared at one another, then hurried to her. Tears were glimmering in her eyes. "She can't find them! Mrs. Taylor can't find my gowns!"

Mrs. Taylor came hurrying in from the pressing room where the ready-to-go gowns were usually kept. "Donna, don't worry now, they have to be here somewhere. Relax, I'll keep looking."

Donna threw herself into Brendan's arms, moaning that her whole wedding was being destroyed. Kaitlin glanced at him over her cousin's head, then turned, determined to search the place herself. She wandered into the rear of the store, then found that she was in a long hallway hung with endless rows of gowns. She followed it back, toward the alley behind the store.

Then she heard the whispering. "Let's go. Now!"

She pushed through the last of the gowns. The back door was open, and a small panel truck was parked beside it. The sliding door of the truck was open, too.

There were no words written on the truck, Kaitlin realized. Nothing that advertised the bridal shop.

And the man loading it was doing so quickly. Very quickly. Looking over his shoulder now and then.

She gasped as she saw the last of the load being thrown on top. Five of them—the color of the dresses for Donna's bridal party—and a wedding gown.

Donna's wedding gown!

"Hey!" she protested. She went tearing after the truck. One of the two men loading it was just pulling down the sliding door.

"Stop! You can't take those! Those are our gowns!" she cried.

Then she saw the two of them exchange glances. One was tall and dark, the other was small and fair.

"What are we gonna do, Spike?" the short one asked the older, dark-haired man.

Spike swore.

Footsteps sounded in the hall, and Kaitlin spun, praying it was Brendan, and that he could make the men give the gowns back.

"Get her, Henry, that's what!" Spike said quickly.

"What?" she gasped. Then she realized the obvious. These men didn't work for the shop. They were stealing the wedding gowns!

And now they were planning on taking *her*, too.

"No!" she gasped and turned to flee.

Fingers wound into her hair. She opened her mouth to scream, but a hand clamped down hard over her mouth. And then she was lifted up and sent flying head first into the pile of wedding gowns.

Her head cracked against something, and the world grew dark for a moment. She was only dimly aware when the door was closed.

Spike and Henry were in the back with her, she realized a moment later. She tried to rise, tried to scream, tried to throw herself against the sliding door. Spike made a flying leap for her legs as the truck jerked into the traffic, and she went down again, half-smothered by the gowns.

"Get her hands!" Spike roared to Henry.

Pudgy little Henry did so, even though Kaitlin fought and tried to bite. With Spike sitting on her legs, nothing she could do was much good.

It was only when her hands and ankles were tied that she panicked. Absolutely panicked. She had heard something about a ring of people who stole bridal gowns in the north and sold them in the south. Donna had told Barbara about it.

And now she was in the middle of it. She was in a truck, going only God knew where, and she was tied hand and foot.

Chills seized her; she shivered violently. They could kill her.

She opened her mouth, gasping for air, desperate to scream.

"Gag her," Spike ordered flatly.

And a grubby handkerchief was tied over her mouth, so tightly that she could scarcely stand the pain. She couldn't barely breathe, and the world was darkening again.

Brendan reached the back of the shop just in time to see the plain white truck disappearing. He hadn't seen Kaitlin; he hadn't heard her.

But when he looked down, he saw one of the little faux-pearl teardrops she had been wearing in her ears. He swore, catching sight of the license plate and watching the direction the truck had chosen, then went tearing through the shop.

"Call the cops," he told Donna quickly, scratching out the license number.

"Thieves have my dresses!" Donna cried.

"They have more than your dresses," Brendan warned her. "They have your maid of honor!"

He didn't wait for any of her questions but went running out the front door to his car. He revved it and went jerking into the street. He nearly hit a garbage can, then gritted his teeth hard, his heart thudding, when he had to slow to allow an old lady to pass.

Damn Kaitlin! She didn't think!

He was so mad at her he wanted to explode!

Then he realized that he wasn't mad, he was just scared as hell. He'd waited all this time to see her. All these weeks. He'd wanted to give her some space.

And now...

Who knew what the hell was happening!

He turned another corner, burning rubber. And there, heading onto the highway, was the truck.

He increased his speed and followed it.

They were heading to the countryside, he realized. Passing from town to town.

Where the hell were the police? he wondered. He had been driving forever. No, he admitted, glancing at his watch. Only about fifteen minutes.

Then the truck turned off the highway and, before long, headed up a dirt road. Brendan forced himself to slow down, then he followed, too.

And there, behind a high row of trees, was a long line of warehouses. The truck pulled up to the first.

Brendan parked under the trees and sat for a moment, gritting his teeth. He wished to hell he had some kind of weapon. A gun, preferably. The police were nowhere around. And Kaitlin was in there.

He got out of the car. Hell, he liked to think he'd done more than learn how to sail in the Navy.

He moved quietly toward the building and slipped around the side. And then he found a window.

They were arguing about her. They had her propped up in a chair, her hands and feet tied, the filthy gag still in her mouth. And Spike had a gun. He was waving it around, fighting with Henry and another man, Sam, the driver.

Sam didn't want to hurt her. "I ain't going to jail for murder one!"

"I ain't going to jail at all, but if we don't get rid of her, we're all going to rot. Hell, we truss her up, blow her away and sink her in concrete. No one will ever be the wiser," Spike said.

"You're disgusting!" Henry told him.

She wasn't going to cry, Kaitlin determined. She wasn't going to panic anymore. What good would it do? She couldn't even begin to move. She just had to pray that Henry and Sam would have the deciding influence. Oh, God! How had she gotten into this?

Tears stung her eyes despite herself.

Stubby little blond Henry was looking at her with sympathy. Spike started to say something about blowing her away, and Henry exploded.

"Not here, Spike, you hear me? Not here!" And he caught Spike's arm and dragged him down a corridor, with Sam close on their heels.

Kaitlin closed her eyes and tried to loosen the ties around her wrists. Absurdly, she thought that it wouldn't matter if she chafed her wrists. They were wearing gloves for the wedding.

They can bury me in gloves, too, she thought.

Oh, she was going to be sick....

Don't panic, don't panic....

Brendan, I love you. I'll never get to tell you, but I'd answer yes to anything. I don't care if we ever marry again. I don't give a damn about a wedding, I'd live with you. I'd follow you. I'd forgive you. I'd love you.

There was suddenly someone behind her, someone with a knife. A little switchblade type thing; she could hear it as it snapped open. A moan sounded in her throat.

"Shh! It's me!" warned a voice.

And then she sensed it. The clean scent of his cologne, and another scent that was all man, the man she loved. She wasn't going to be stabbed in the back. It was Brendan. Relief almost made her black out.

The rope was nearly shredded. It wasn't a switchblade, she realized, just a little pocket knife. He loosened her gag. "Oh, Brendan!" she murmured. Then, "Hurry. There's three of them. Spike, Henry and Sam. Spike's the mean guy with the gun. Henry's the short, paunchy one, the easiest to get past, I think. And—"

There were footsteps coming toward them. Brendan swore and slipped the gag over her mouth as Henry appeared in the room, Spike and Sam behind him.

Brendan left Kaitlin and swaggered into the center of the room. "She's a real pain in the butt, isn't she?" he demanded, before they could speak.

Spike had his gun pointed at Brendan's chest. "Who the hell are you?" he demanded.

"I'm here to make a deal," Brendan told him, hoping the other man wouldn't stop to wonder how he had known where "here" was.

"What?" Henry demanded.

"Yeah, I want some of these down San Antonio way. Fifty-fifty. I'm telling you, I can sell them right and left, no questions asked."

Spike swaggered up to him, wagging the gun beneath his nose. It was a .38, an old police issue, probably stolen, Brendan decided.

What difference did that make? he wondered. No matter where it had come from, it was a lethal weapon.

But Spike didn't seem to be comfortable with it. Yeah, he waved it around. But Brendan was almost certain that he'd never used it on a human being. Spike was more talk than action.

"I want the girl, too."

Spike shook his head. "You can't—"

"I'm glad you tied her up. She's Irish, you know. She's got one of those god-awful tempers. And she's trouble. Lots of it. But she kind of grows on you. Now, I'll give you big money for the dresses, but I want the girl thrown in, too.''

Henry turned to Spike. ''These are going to be as hot as tamales! Let's give him the damn things—and the girl, too.''

Spike wasn't looking at Brendan, who realized that this was his chance. He slammed his arm down in a heavy chop on Spike's. The .38 went flying.

He punched Spike, who went down, but then Sam came after him, trying to butt him like a bull. He sidestepped Sam and chopped down on his neck and shoulders. Sam went down, too, but then Henry was running for the gun.

Brendan made a dive for him, caught his ankles and brought him down heavily. He made an oomph sound and went still, but Brendan knew that Spike was up and coming after him again. He had to reach the gun himself.

Then he didn't need to. Kaitlin was up, the ties discarded, her mouth free from the gag. She went racing past him, sweeping down on the gun just as Spike began to get near it.

She spun around, furious, aiming it at Spike's heart. ''I don't know how to use one of these things, and I'm nervous as hell, but I think you just tug on the trigger here. You wanted to blow me away, so if you take one more step in my direction, I swear I'll blow *you* right to kingdom come!''

Spike must have believed her, because he went dead still. Brendan rose, walked over to her, reached for the .38 and smiled. "That was pretty good. But I do know how to use that thing, so do you want to let me have it?"

She gave him a brilliant smile and handed him the gun.

And then she passed out cold, not falling hard, just wilting slowly to the ground.

Brendan heard the sirens at the same moment. At last, he thought gratefully.

All in all, Kaitlin decided later, it was a wonderful wedding. A beautiful wedding. The stuff that dreams were made of. Eventually.

First she'd had to bargain with the police, flirting outrageously with a young officer to get him to give her Donna's gowns when they should have been evidence. And, of course, Brendan had been furious with her for flirting.

Then they'd split up. She'd helped Donna dress, along with the other bridesmaids. Then the limo had come for them, and they'd sipped champagne on the way to the church.

Then came the next snag.

There was no groom. Donna's father found out that the driver had gone to the wrong town, so there was no way on earth the groom and his best man could show up at the church anywhere near on time.

But they did. Brendan and Bill arrived in an old pickup truck, smiling and proud of themselves. Cheers went up, and the wedding was on. And it was beautiful, just beautiful, with Brendan and Kaitlin waging a discreetly silent war over the placement of Donna's train.

Then her cousin was wed, and they were leaving the church amidst the glow of candles.

Someone had forgotten the champagne for the limo ride to the reception, but no one seemed to mind. The embarrassed driver offered them a six-pack of Canadian beer, and they all laughed and decided that they'd just have to smell like a brewery when they arrived at the hall.

The flower girl didn't quite make it across the floor when she was announced at the reception—her daddy was in the band, so she stopped and swayed to the music. But Kaitlin, smiling, knew that it was part of the beauty, part of the humanity and part of the wonder that Donna would get to remember all her life.

Suddenly she thought she was going to cry.

Gram had always had it right. It wasn't the wedding that mattered. It was the marriage. And any way it was done, it was the vows that mattered, not the tinsel. It was people, and it was love....

The first dance was announced. Donna danced with Bill, then with her father. And then Kaitlin was able to dance with Brendan.

But there were so many people there. They weren't able to talk. Not for a long time.

Not until Donna had tossed the bouquet—aiming straight for Kaitlin. And she had caught it.

And Bill somehow managed to slam Brendan right in the forehead with Donna's garter. He had to catch it; the darned thing fell right in his hands.

And so Brendan was on his knees before Kaitlin again, as he had been so many years before, his fingers moving deliciously over her stockinged thigh. She knew that she was smiling, and that her eyes were glittering, and he probably didn't need an answer to anything anymore.

He must know that she loved him, that she always had.

Finally the garter was on her leg, and everyone was cheering and laughing.

"Think I can get it all in with this one shot?" he asked her, gazing into her eyes. He was striking in his black tux and tails, but it was his crooked smile that seized her heart. That and the huskiness in his voice.

"Get what in with one shot?"

"Well, you know, it just always seems that I'm on my knees for you. Asking you to marry me."

"What?" she whispered.

"I want you to marry me again, Kaitlin. I've never stopped loving you. I never will. And I believe with all my heart that we belong together. I want a family now, Kaitlin. I want to go sailing with you, and I want you to tell me all about your problems at work. And most of all, I want to sleep beside you, to hold you. I want to see the blue of your eyes every single morning. I want to cherish the time that we have left. I want to give you the wedding of your dreams this time. I promise that I'll never shut you out again. I'll probably still have a bad temper, but then, you do, too, so we should be able to deal with that, as long as we always talk. I never want to lose you again, so I know I'll always be there. I'll give you the biggest diamond you've ever seen—''

"No!" she cried. She had forgotten where they were. She slid off the chair to her knees and caught his fingers, lacing them through her own. "No, I don't want a different diamond, I want the old one—''

"You still have it?"

"Yes!"

"And the wedding ring?"

"That, too."

"I have mine, too. And I've asked your father for you all over again, I thought that our parents had a right to know, and—''

"I love you, Brendan," she interrupted, and kissed him. And then, when a loud roar went up, Kaitlin realized at last that they had one hell of an audience.

"Excuse us, will you?" Brendan said casually. He stood, pulling her up with him, and smiled, then swept her from the hall and ran through the corridors with her until he found an empty room.

And, once inside, he kissed her.

Open-mouthed, sweetly, hotly passionate. The kind of kiss that had made her melt at eighteen.

The kind of kiss that made her melt right now. And then, trembling, she was in his arms, trying to say all the things she had to tell him.

"I don't need a big wedding. I never did, really. I just didn't realize it. Oh, Brendan, I don't care, I don't—"

"I care," he insisted, his eyes gleaming. "This is the last time I want to marry you, Kaitlin. I want it to be perfect. I found out that since we were married by a justice of the peace the first time, we can get a dispensation to be married in the church."

"Brendan, I don't care—"

"Kaitlin, I do. And think how good we'll be at weddings by the time we get to our own! We still have to see Barbara and Joe legally wed, then we can get to our own."

"Oh, Brendan . . ."

"You haven't answered me yet, Kaitlin."

Very, very slowly, she smiled, her arms looped around his neck, her eyes radiant, dazzling. "Okay, a big wedding. On one condition."

"What's that?"

"You don't disappear for almost a month again. We, er . . ."

"We what?"

"We get to fool around in the meantime. Maybe we could even go ahead and start thinking family a wee bit before the ceremony, as Gram might say."

"With her teeth in," Brendan agreed.

Kaitlin laughed and, once again, he took her in his arms.

She was certain in that very moment that their vows were sealed. She didn't need the wedding. She never had. She needed Brendan. She loved Brendan.

And she had never really lost him. . . .

But weddings were wonderful, she decided long moments later.

At this one, she had found her way back home.

Epilogue

Okay, so it was worth it.

Yes, definitely worth it, Brendan decided.

This just might be the most beautiful wedding he had ever seen, and it was his own.

The church was dressed in flowers, red and white, and regal candles burned atop elegant long brass poles attached to every pew. Kaitlin's mother and his own were seated to the glorious notes of "Ave Maria," and then, as the organ continued to play, their wedding party began to appear.

First came her little cousin, Brandy, in the elegant cream and black dress Kaitlin had chosen, her red curls adorned with a tiara of flowers. Then her junior bridesmaid walked down the aisle with the ring bearer, handsome in his very traditional tux. The ushers escorted her bridesmaids and her two matrons of honor, Donna and Barbara.

And then came Kaitlin.

Escorted on her father's arm, she was achingly beautiful. She wore a traditional gown, but it was a soft dove gray, not white. Yet Brendan had never seen anything more elegant. Seed pearls had been sewn into a beautiful design, along with soft, glimmering sequins. A veil covered her face, and a sweeping train followed behind her. Her hair was free and flowing down her back, just shaded by the gauze of her veil. The gown's bodice was medieval, the sleeves long and tapering, and the veil was held in place by a narrow crown of seed pearls and flowers.

And yet, most beautiful of all were her eyes. Sapphire blue that day, glimmering through the gauze of her veil until she reached the altar. Then her father lifted her veil, and the two of them smiled at one another with pride and love and just a hint of tears.

Someone sniffed loudly. Either her mother or Brendan's, she was certain.

And then her father was handing her over to him, and the love in her eyes touched him. Somewhere deep inside his heart, he felt a quiver. And even before the service began, long before they exchanged their vows, he knew that this time it would last forever.

His voice was steady and firm as they exchanged their vows. Hers was crystal clear, but her finger trembled slightly when he slipped on her wedding ring.

It was the same ring he had given her twelve years before. She had kept it, just as he had kept the ring she had given him. Perhaps the diamond was small. It didn't matter to either of them. What did matter was that they both still had the rings. And they both knew that no other rings could possibly do.

They pledged their love. They knelt, they rose, Barbara adjusted Kaitlin's train.

There was another sniff from somewhere. Brendan smiled. Gram. Lizzie Boyle Rosen. She was right behind them, he knew, next to Brendan's mom, her arm linked through her beloved Al's. Bless you, Lizzie, Brendan thought. You were always rooting for me, weren't you?

He heard the words and the music. But most of all, he felt Kaitlin beside him. Felt her hand when they touched, felt the trembling inside her. Breathed in the sweetness of her perfume, and met the shining happiness in her eyes.

To love, honor and cherish . . .

He smiled, and as Father Mulraney said that he could kiss the bride, he swept her into his arms to a cacophony of applause.

She was his wife again. Kaitlin, with her laughter, her spirit, her beauty, her sky-blue eyes and waves of strawberry curls. With her temper, too, but with all her wisdom and, most importantly, all her love.

It had been beautiful. A perfect wedding, he thought as he tasted her kiss. The wedding she had always seen in her dreams.

It was perfect for him, too. The wedding he had envisioned when he had been so much younger. If only Sean had been there.

Even as that thought touched his heart, she broke from his embrace, and smiled at him radiantly, her fingers still locked in his own.

Once again he felt the trembling deep within his heart. Her emotions were so easily read within the blue beauty of her eyes. Her lips were curved into a smile of such sweet warmth that even now he felt a growing wonder that it could be for him.

It almost seemed that there was a whisper breathed against his ear. Sean's whisper. "You're lucky, cousin. You've got love. When you've got love, you've got everything."

He had to kiss her again. He pulled her into his arms, and there was a burst of applause as their lips met and he kissed her for another eternity.

When he released her, there was laughter in her eyes, and just a hint of tears. Then he took her hand, the music started, and he led her down the aisle and out of the church.

Before the others could follow too closely behind him, he swept her into his arms, delicately planting a kiss on her forehead.

"I love you, Kaitlin O'Herlihy," he told her.

"Oh, Brendan! I love you, too, so much! You gave me everything! Everything I wanted!"

Barbara and Joe were behind them by then. Joe was claiming a kiss from the bride, while Barbara congratulated Brendan and hugged him warmly. And then Barbara and Donna were hugging Kaitlin, and Joe and Bill were there to pump Brendan's hand, while the others were pouring out of the church.

So many good friends and relatives to greet them.

Lizzie and Al. Brendan's mother, with tears in her eyes. His father, proud, pleased. His cousins, her cousins. His family, her family.

Their family, now. And all their friends.

Everyone told them what a perfect wedding it had been. And it had been perfect, he thought, closing his eyes for just a second as a smile teased his lips. It seemed that Sean had made this wedding. In wisdom, in spirit.

Before anyone could part them again, he found his bride's hand and pulled her into his arms. "No," he told her. "You gave *me* everything. I have your love, Kaitlin, and love is everything."

Just for good measure, he kissed her long and hard again, heedless of those around them.

They would just have to wait...because love was everything.

* * * * *

Double your reading pleasure this fall with two Award of Excellence titles written by two of your favorite authors.

Available in September

DUNCAN'S BRIDE
by Linda Howard
Silhouette Intimate Moments #349

Mail-order bride Madelyn Patterson was nothing like what Reese Duncan expected—and everything he needed.

Available in October

THE COWBOY'S LADY
by Debbie Macomber
Silhouette Special Edition #626

The Montana cowboy wanted a little lady at his beck and call—the "lady" in question saw things differently....

These titles have been selected to receive a special laurel—the Award of Excellence. Look for the distinctive emblem on the cover. It lets you know there's something truly wonderful inside! DUN-1

Silhouette Special Edition®

**Appearing in October
for a return engagement, Nora Roberts's
bestselling 1988 miniseries featuring**

THE O'HURLEYS!
Nora Roberts

Book 1 **THE LAST HONEST WOMAN** *Abby's Story*
Book 2 **DANCE TO THE PIPER** *Maddy's Story*
Book 3 **SKIN DEEP** *Chantel's Story*

And making his debut in a brand-new title, a very special
leading man . . . Trace O'Hurley!

Book 4 **WITHOUT A TRACE** *Trace's Tale*

In 1988, Nora Roberts introduced THE O'HURLEYS!—a close-knit
family of entertainers whose early travels spanned the country. The
beautiful triplet sisters and their mysterious brother each experience
the triumphant joy and passion only true love can bring, in four books
you will remember long after the last pages are turned.

Don't miss this captivating miniseries in October—a special collec-
tor's edition available wherever paperbacks are sold.

Take 4 bestselling love stories FREE

Plus get a FREE surprise gift!